Ari

D0646292

by
Brre studys

Enjoy all of
Beverly Cleary's books

FEATURING RAMONA QUIMBY:

Beezus and Ramona

Ramona the Pest

Ramona the Brave

Ramona and Her Father

Ramona and Her Mother

Ramona Quimby, Age 8

Ramona Forever

Ramona's World

FEATURING HENRY HUGGINS:

Henry Huggins

Henry and Beezus

Henry and Ribsy

Henry and the Paper Route

Henry and the Clubhouse

Ribsy

FEATURING RALPH MOUSE:

The Mouse and the Motorcycle

Runaway Ralph

Ralph S. Mouse

MORE GREAT FICTION BY BEVERLY CLEARY:

Ellen Tebbits

Otis Spofford

Fifteen

The Luckiest Girl

Jean and Johnny

Emily's Runaway Imagination

Sister of the Bride

Mitch and Amy

Socks

Dear Mr. Henshaw

Muggie Maggie

Strider

Two Times the Fun

AND DON'T MISS BEVERLY CLEARY'S AUTOBIOGRAPHIES:

A Girl from Yamhill

My Own Two Feet

Beverly Cleary

Ramona
THE
Brave

ILLUSTRATED BY
Tracy Dockray

HarperTrophy®
An Imprint of HarperCollinsPublishers

Ramona the Brave

Copyright © 1975 by Beverly Cleary

All rights reserved. No part of this book may be used or reproduced in any manner
whatsoever without written permission except in the case of brief quotations embodied
in critical articles and reviews. Manufactured in China. For information address
HarperCollins Children's Books, a division of HarperCollins Publishers,
10 East 53rd Street, New York, NY 10022.

ISBN 978-0-06-201564-8

Typography by Amy Ryan

10 11 12 13 14 SCP 10 9 8 7 6 5 4 3 2 1

contents

1
Trouble in The Park

Ramona Quimby, brave and fearless, was half running, half skipping to keep up with her big sister Beatrice on their way home from the park. She had never seen her sister's cheeks so flushed with anger as they were this August afternoon. Ramona was sticky from heat and grubby from landing in the sawdust at the foot of the slides, but she was proud of herself. When Mrs. Quimby had sent the girls to the park for an hour, because she had an errand to do—an important errand, she hinted—she told Beezus, as Beatrice was called, to look after Ramona.

And what had happened? For the first time in her six years Ramona had looked after Beezus, who was supposed to be the responsible one. *Bossy* was a better word, Ramona sometimes thought. But not today. Ramona had stepped forward and defended her sister for a change.

"Beezus," said Ramona, panting, "slow down."

Beezus, clutching her library book in her sweaty hand, paid no attention. The clang of rings, the steady pop of tennis balls against asphalt, and the shouts of children grew fainter as the girls approached their house on Klickitat Street.

Ramona hoped their mother would be

home from her errand, whatever it was. She couldn't wait to tell what had happened and how she had defended her big sister. Her mother would be so proud, and so would her father when he came home from work and heard the story. "Good for you, Ramona," he would say. "That's the old fight!" Brave little Ramona.

Fortunately, the car was in the garage and Mrs. Quimby was in the living room when the girls burst into the house. "Why, Beezus," said their mother, when she saw the flushed and sweaty faces of her daughters, one angry and one triumphant.

Beezus blinked to hold back the tears in her eyes.

"Ramona, what happened to Beezus?" Mrs. Quimby was alarmed.

"Don't *ever* call me Beezus again!" Beezus's voice was fierce.

Mrs. Quimby looked at Ramona for the explanation, and Ramona was eager to give it. Usually Beezus was the one who explained what had happened to Ramona, how she had dropped her ice-cream cone on the sidewalk and cried when Beezus would not let her pick it up, or how she tried, in spite of the rules, to go down a slide

4

headfirst and had landed on her face in the sawdust. Now Ramona was going to have a turn. She took a deep breath and prepared to tell her tale. "Well, when we went to the park, I slid on the slides awhile and Beezus sat on a bench reading her library book. Then I saw an empty swing. A big swing, not a baby swing over the wading pool, and I thought since I'm going to be in the first grade next month I should swing on the big swings. Shouldn't I, Mama?"

"Yes, of course." Mrs. Quimby was impatient. "Please, go on with the story. What happened to Beezus?"

"Well, I climbed up in the swing," Ramona continued, "only my feet wouldn't touch the ground because there was this big hollow under the swing." Ramona recalled how she had longed to swing until the chains went slack in her hands and her toes pointed to the tops of the fir trees, but she sensed that she had better hurry up with her story or her mother would ask Beezus to tell it. Ramona never liked to lose an audience. "And I said, 'Beezus, push me,' and some big boys, big bad boys, heard me and one of them said—" Ramona, eager to be the one to tell the story but reluctant to repeat the words, hesitated.

"Said what?" Mrs. Quimby was baffled. "Said what, Ramona? Beezus, what did he say?"

Beezus wiped the back of her wrist across her eyes and tried. "He said, 'J-j-j—'"

Eagerness to beat her sister at telling what had happened overcame Ramona's reluctance. "He said, 'Jesus, Beezus!'" Ramona looked up at her mother, waiting for her to be shocked. Instead she merely looked surprised and—could it be?—amused.

"And that is why I never, never, *never* want to be called Beezus again!" said Beezus.

"And all the other boys began to say it,

too," said Ramona, warming to her story now that she was past the bad part. "Oh, Mama, it was just awful. It was *terrible*. All those big awful boys! They kept saying, 'Jesus, Beezus' and 'Beezus, Jesus.' I jumped out of the swing, and I told them—"

Here Beezus interrupted. Anger once more replaced tears. "And then Ramona had to get into the act. Do you know what she did? She jumped out of the swing and preached a sermon! Nobody wants a little sister tagging around preaching sermons to a bunch of boys. And they weren't that big either. They were just trying to act big."

Ramona was stunned by this view of her behavior. How unfair of Beezus when she had been so brave. And the boys *had* seemed big to her.

Mrs. Quimby spoke to Beezus as if Ramona were not present. "A sermon! You must be joking."

Ramona tried again. "Mama, I—"

Beezus was not going to give her little sister a chance to speak. "No, I'm not joking. And then Ramona stuck her thumbs in her ears, waggled her fingers, and stuck out her tongue. I just about died, I was so embarrassed."

Ramona was suddenly subdued. She had thought Beezus was angry at the boys, but now it turned out she was angry with her little sister, too. Maybe angrier. Ramona was used to being considered a little pest, and she knew she sometimes was a pest, but this was something different. She felt as if she were standing aside looking at herself. She saw a stranger, a funny little six-year-old girl with straight brown hair, wearing grubby shorts and an old T-shirt, inherited from Beezus, which had Camp Namanu printed across the front. A silly little girl embarrassing her sister so much that Beezus was ashamed of her. And she had been proud of

herself because she thought she was being brave. Now it turned out that she was not brave. She was silly and embarrassing. Ramona's confidence in herself was badly shaken. She tried again. "Mama, I—"

Mrs. Quimby felt her older daughter deserved all her attention. "Were they boys you know?" she asked.

"Sort of," said Beezus with a sniff. "They go to our school, and now when school starts all the boys in the sixth grade will be saying it. Sixth-grade boys are *awful*."

"They will have forgotten by then." Mrs. Quimby tried to be reassuring. Beezus sniffed again.

"Mama, I think we *should* stop calling her Beezus." Even though her feelings were hurt, and her confidence shaken, Ramona had a reason of her own for trying to help Beezus.

Whenever someone asked Beezus where she got such an unusual nickname, Beezus always answered that it came from Ramona. When she was little she couldn't say Beatrice. Now that Ramona was about to enter first grade, she did not like to remember there was a time when she could not pronounce her sister's name.

"Just because I have an Aunt Beatrice, I

don't see why I have to be named Beatrice, too," said Beezus. "Nobody else has a name like Beatrice."

"You wouldn't want a name like everyone else's," Mrs. Quimby pointed out.

"I know," agreed Beezus, "but *Beatrice*."

"Yuck," said Ramona, trying to be helpful, but her mother frowned at her. "How about Trissy?" she suggested hastily.

Beezus was rude. "Don't be dumb. Then they would call me Sissy Trissy or something. Boys in the sixth grade think up *awful* names."

"Nobody ever calls me anything but Ramona Kimona." Ramona could not help thinking that an awful nickname might be interesting to have. "Why not just be Beatrice? Nobody can think up a bad nickname for Beatrice."

"Yes, I guess you're right," agreed Beezus. "I'll have to be plain old Beatrice with her plain old brown hair."

"I think Beatrice is fancy," said Ramona, who also had plain old brown hair but did not take it so hard. Agreeing with Beezus—Beatrice—gave Ramona a cozy feeling, as if something unusually pleasant had taken place. Beezus honored Ramona with a watery smile, forgiving her, at least for the moment, for preaching a sermon.

Ramona felt secure and happy. Agreeing was so pleasant she wished she and her sister could agree more often. Unfortunately, there were many things to disagree about—whose turn it was to feed Picky-picky, the old yellow cat, who should change the paper under Picky-picky's dish, whose washcloth had been left sopping in the bathtub because someone had not wrung it out, and whose dirty underwear had been left in whose half of the room. Ramona always said Beezus—Beatrice—was bossy, because she was older. Beatrice said Ramona always got her own way, because she was the baby and because she always made a fuss. For the moment all this was forgotten.

Mrs. Quimby smiled to see her girls at peace with one another. "Don't worry, Beatrice. If the boys tease you, just hold your head high and ignore them. When they see they can't tease you, they will stop."

The two sisters exchanged a look of complete understanding. They both knew this was the sort of advice easy for adults to give but difficult for children to follow. If the boys remembered, Beezus might have to listen to "Jesus, Beezus" for months before they gave up.

"By the way, Ramona," said Mrs. Quimby, as Beatrice went off to the bathroom to splash cold water on her face, "what did you say to the boys in the park?"

Ramona, who had flopped back on the couch, sat up straight. "I told them they were not supposed to take the name of the Lord in vain," she said in her most proper Sunday School voice. "That's what my Sunday School teacher said."

"Oh, I see," said Mrs. Quimby. "And what did they say to that?"

Ramona was chagrined because she knew her mother was amused, and Ramona did not like anyone to be amused when she was serious. "Wasn't I right? That's what I learned in Sunday School." She was filled with uncertainty by her mother's amusement, as well as by her sister's anger over the incident.

"Of course, you were right, dear, although I don't suppose a bunch of boys would pay much attention." Mrs. Quimby's lips were not smiling, but amusement lingered in her eyes. "How did the boys answer?"

Ramona's confidence wilted completely. She was seeing that little girl in the park who was not the heroine she thought she was after all. "They laughed," Ramona admitted in a small voice, feeling sorry for herself. Poor little Ramona, laughed at and picked on. Nobody understood how she felt. Nobody understood what it was like to be six years old and the littlest one in the family unless you counted old Picky-picky, and even he was ten years old.

Mrs. Quimby gave Ramona a big hug. "Well, it's all over now," she said. "Run along and play, but *please* don't play Brick Factory this afternoon."

"Don't worry, Mother. I don't have any bricks left."

Ramona felt that her mother should be able to see that running along and playing was impossible on a hot summer afternoon when everyone Ramona's age had gone to the beach or the mountains or to visit a grandmother. The two weeks the Quimbys had spent in a borrowed mountain cabin in

July now seemed a long time away. Who was she supposed to play with?

Summer was boring. Long and boring. No bricks left for the game of Brick Factory, which she and her friend Howie had invented, nobody to play with, and Beezus with her nose in a book all day.

Not having any place to run along to, Ramona sat looking at her mother, thinking that her fresh haircut and touch of eye shadow made her look unusually nice this afternoon. She wondered if her mother would tell her father about the incident in the park and if they would have a good laugh over it when they thought Ramona could not hear. She hoped not. She did not want her father to laugh at her.

Seeing her mother looking so nice made Ramona recall the reason for the trip to the park. "What was your errand that you didn't want to drag us along on?" she asked.

Mrs. Quimby smiled a different smile, exasperating and mysterious. "Sh-h-h," she said, her finger on her lips. "It's a secret, and wild horses couldn't drag it out of me."

Ramona found secrets hard to bear. "Tell me, Mama! Mama, *please* tell me." She threw her arms around her mother, who had a good smell of clean clothes and perfumed

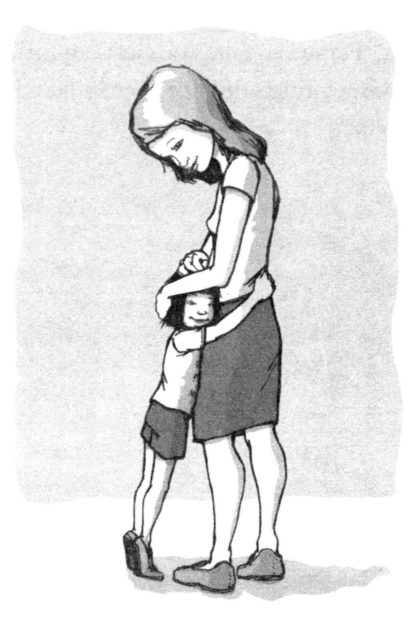

soap. "Please, please, *please!*" Learning a big juicy secret would help make up for Ramona's unhappy afternoon.

Mrs. Quimby shook her head.

"Pretty please with a lump of sugar on it?" Ramona felt she could not bear not knowing this very minute.

"If I told you, it wouldn't be a secret anymore," said Mrs. Quimby.

That, Ramona felt, was just about the most exasperating sentence ever spoken by a grown-up.

2

Mrs. Quimby's Secret

Mrs. Quimby, wearing a dress instead of old slacks, had gone off on another mysterious errand. She promised not to be away long, and Beezus and Ramona promised to stay out of trouble while she was out, a promise easier for Beezus to keep than for Ramona. Beezus disappeared with a book into the room the girls shared. Ramona settled herself at the kitchen table with paper and crayons to draw a picture of the cat on the label of a can of Puss'n Boots cat food. Ramona loved that jaunty booted cat, so different from old Picky-picky, who spent most of his time napping on Beezus's bed.

The house was quiet. Ramona worked happily, humming a tune from a television commercial. She used a pencil to draw cat fur, because she could draw finer lines with it than she could with a crayon. She used her crayons for Puss'n Boots's clothes, but when she came to his boots, she discovered her red crayon was missing. Most likely she had left it in her room.

"Beezus, have you seen my red crayon?" The girls had made an agreement that Ramona could call her sister Beezus at home, but in public she had better remember to call her Beatrice or look out!

"Um-hm." Without looking up from her

book, Beezus waved her hand in the direction of Ramona's bed.

Peace between the sisters could not last. Ramona saw the broken remains of her red crayon lying in the middle of her bed. "Who broke my crayon?" she demanded.

"You shouldn't leave your crayon on other people's beds where it can get sat on." Beezus did not even bother to look up from her book.

Ramona found this answer most annoying. "You should look where you sit," she said, "and you don't have to be so bossy."

"This is my bed." Beezus glanced at her sister. "You have your own half of the room."

"I don't have anyplace to put anything."

"Pooh," said Beezus. "You're just careless and messy."

Ramona was indignant. "I am not careless and messy!" Picky-picky woke up, leaped from Beezus's bed, and departed, tail held

straight. Picky-picky often made it plain he did not care for Ramona.

"Yes, you are," said Beezus. "You don't hang up your clothes, and you leave your toys all over."

"Just because the clothes bar is easy for you to reach," said Ramona, "and you think you're too big for toys." To show her sister that she did pick up her things, she laid the

pieces of her broken crayon in her drawer on top of her underwear. She had lost interest in crayoning. She did not want to color boots with the rough ends of a broken crayon.

"Besides," said Beezus, who did not like to be interrupted when she was deep in a good book, "you're a pest."

Pest was a fighting word to Ramona, because it was unfair. She was not a pest, at least not all the time. She was only littler than anyone else in the family, and no matter how hard she tried, she could not catch up. "Don't you call me a pest," she shouted, "or I'll tell Mama you have a lipstick hidden in your drawer."

Beezus finally laid down her book. "Ramona Geraldine Quimby!" Her voice and manner were fierce. "You're nothing but a snoop and a tattletale!"

Ramona had gone too far. "I wasn't snooping. I was looking for a safety pin," she explained, adding, as if she were a very good girl, "and anyway I haven't told Mama *yet*."

Beezus gave her sister a look of disgust. "Ramona, grow up!"

Ramona lost all patience. *"Can't you see I'm trying?"* she yelled at the top of her voice. People were always telling her to grow up. What did they think she was trying to do?

"Try harder," was Beezus's heartless answer. "And stop bothering me when I've come to the good part in my book."

Ramona shoved aside her stuffed animals and threw herself on her bed with *Wild Animals of Africa*, a book with interesting pictures but without the three grown-up words, *gas*, *motel*, and *burger*, which she had taught herself from signs but was unable to find in books. The book fell open to the

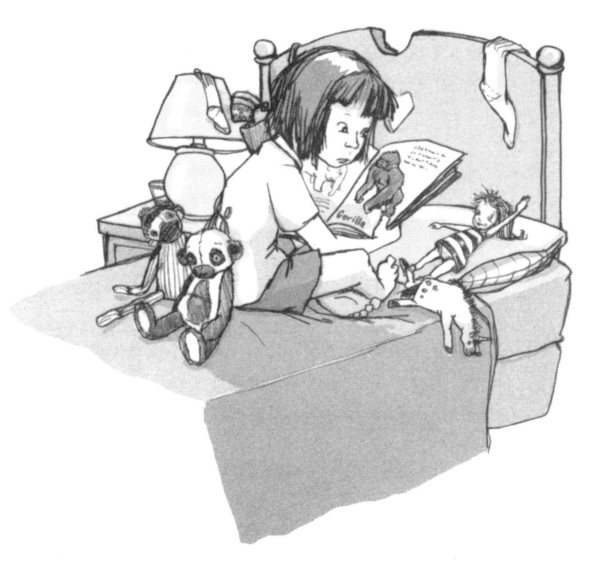

page that she had looked at most often, a full-page colored photograph of a gorilla. Ramona stared briefly and intensely at the gorilla, taking in his mighty body covered with blue-black hair, his tiny eyes, the dark caves of his nostrils, his long and powerful arms with hands like leather that hung almost to the ground. With a satisfying shiver, Ramona slammed the book shut. She wouldn't want to meet that old gorilla coming down the street or swinging through the trees of the park. She let the book fall open again. The gorilla was still there, staring out of the page with fierce little eyes. Ramona slammed the gorilla in again. When Ramona was bored, she enjoyed scaring herself.

"Ramona, do you have to keep slamming that book?" asked Beezus.

Ramona slammed the book a few more times to show her sister she could slam the book all she wanted to.

"Pest," said Beezus, to show Ramona she could call her a pest if she wanted to.

"I am not a pest!" yelled Ramona.

"You are too a pest!" Beezus yelled back.

Ha, thought Ramona, at least I got you away from your old book. "I'm not a pest, and you're just bossy!" she shouted.

"Silence, varlet," commanded Beezus. "Yonder car approacheth. Our noble mother cometh." People talked like that in the books Beezus was reading lately.

Ramona thought Beezus was showing off. "Don't you call me a bad name!" she shouted, half hoping her mother would hear.

In a moment Mrs. Quimby appeared in the doorway. She looked angry. Beezus shot Ramona an it's-all-your-fault look.

"Girls, you can be heard all over the neighborhood," said Mrs. Quimby.

Ramona sat up and looked virtuous.

"Beezus called me a bad name."

"How do you know?" asked Beezus. "You don't even know what *varlet* means."

Mrs. Quimby took in the two girls on their rumpled beds, Ramona's toys heaped in the corner, the overflowing dresser. Then,

28

when she spoke, she said an astonishing thing. "I don't blame you girls one little bit for bickering so much. This room is much too small for two growing girls, so of course you get on one another's nerves."

The sisters looked at each other and relaxed. Their mother understood.

"Well, we're going to do something about it," Mrs. Quimby continued. "We're going to go ahead and build that extra bedroom onto the house."

Beezus sat up, and this time she was the one to slam her book shut. "Oh, Mother!" she cried. "Are we *really*?"

Ramona understood the stress on that last word. The extra room had been talked about for so long that neither sister believed it would actually be built. Mr. Quimby had drawn plans for knocking out the back of the closet where the vacuum cleaner was kept and extending the house into the backyard just enough to add a small bedroom with the closet-turned-into-a-hall leading to it. Ramona had heard a lot of uninteresting grown-up talk about borrowing money from a bank to pay for it, but nothing had ever come of it. All she understood was that her father worked at something that sounded boring in an office downtown, and there was never quite enough money in the Quimby family. They were certainly not poor, but her parents worried a lot about taxes and college educations.

"Where will we get the money to pay back the bank?" asked Beezus, who understood these things better than Ramona.

Mrs. Quimby smiled, about to make an important announcement. "I have a job that begins as soon as school starts."

"A job!" cried the sisters.

"Yes," said their mother. "I am going to work from nine in the morning till two in the afternoon in Dr. Perry's office. That way I can be here when Ramona gets home from school. And on my way home from talking to Dr. Perry, I stopped at the bank and arranged to borrow the money to pay for the room."

"Oh, Mother!" Beezus was all enthusiasm. Dr. Perry was the woman who had given the girls their checkups and their shots ever since they were born. "Just think! You're going to be liberated!"

Ramona was pleased by the look of amusement that flickered across her mother's face. Ramona wasn't the only one who said things grown-ups thought funny.

"That remains to be seen," said Mrs. Quimby, "and depends on how much help I get from you girls."

"And you'll get to see all the darling babies!" Beezus loved babies and could hardly wait until she was old enough to baby-sit. "Oh, Mother, you're so lucky!"

Mrs. Quimby smiled. "I'm going to be Dr. Perry's bookkeeper. I won't be taking care of babies."

Ramona was less enthusiastic than Beezus. "Who will take care of me if I get sick?" she wanted to know.

"Howie's grandmother," said Mrs. Quimby. "She's always glad to earn a little extra money."

Ramona, who knew all about Howie's grandmother, made up her mind to stay well. "Who will bake cookies?" she asked.

"Oh, cookies." Mrs. Quimby dismissed cookies as unimportant. "We can buy them at the store, or you can bake them from a mix. You're old enough now."

"I might burn myself," said Ramona darkly.

"Not if you are careful." Mrs. Quimby's good spirits could not be budged.

Suddenly Ramona and her sister ex-changed an anxious glance, and each tried to speak faster than the other. "Who gets the new room?" they both wanted to know.

Ramona began to feel unhappy and left out before her mother had a chance to answer. Beezus always got everything, because she was older. Beezus got to stay up later. She got to spend the night at Mary Jane's house and go away to camp. She got most of the new clothes, and when she had outgrown them, they were put away for Ramona. There was no hope.

"Now, girls," said Mrs. Quimby, "don't get all worked up. Your father and I talked it over a long time ago and decided you will take turns. Every six months you will trade."

Ramona had a quick word with God. "Who gets it first?" she asked, anxious again.

Mrs. Quimby smiled. "You do."

"Moth-ther!" wailed Beezus. "Couldn't we at least draw straws?"

Mrs. Quimby shook her head. "Ramona has a point when she says she never gets anything first because she is younger. We thought this time Ramona could be first for a change. Don't you agree that's fair?"

"Yes!" shouted Ramona.

"I guess so," said Beezus.

"Good," said Mrs. Quimby, the matter settled.

"Is a man going to come and really chop a hole in the house?" asked Ramona.

"Next week," said her mother.

Ramona could hardly wait. The summer was no longer boring. Something was going to happen after all. And when school started, she would have something exciting to share with her class for Show and Tell. A hole chopped in the house!

3

The Hole in The House

Although Ramona was standing with her nose pressed against the front window, she was wild with impatience. She was impatient for school to start. She was impatient because no matter how many times her mother telephoned, the workmen had not come to start the new room, and if they did not start the new room, how was Ramona going to astound the first grade by telling them about the hole chopped in the house? She was impatient because she had nothing to do.

"Ramona, how many times do I have to tell you not to rub your nose against the window? You smudge the glass." Mrs. Quimby sounded as if she too looked forward to the beginning of school.

Ramona's answer was, "Mother! Here comes Howie. With bricks!"

"Oh, dear," said Mrs. Quimby.

Ramona ran out to meet Howie, who was trudging down Klickitat Street pulling his little red wagon full of old bricks, the very best kind for playing Brick Factory, because they were old and broken with the corners crumbled away. "Where did you get them?" asked Ramona, who knew how scarce old bricks were in their neighborhood.

"At my other grandmother's," said Howie. "A bulldozer was smashing some old houses so somebody could build a shopping center, and the man told me I could pick up broken bricks."

"Let's get started," said Ramona, running to the garage and returning with two big rocks she and Howie used in playing Brick Factory, a simple but satisfying game. Each grasped a rock in both hands and with it pounded a brick into pieces and the pieces into smithereens. The pounding was hard, tiring work. *Pow! Pow! Pow!* Then they

reduced the smithereens to dust. *Crunch, crunch, crunch.* They were no longer six-year-olds. They were the strongest people in the world. They were giants.

When the driveway was thick with red dust, Ramona dragged out the hose and pretended that a terrible flood was washing away the Brick Factory in a stream of red mud. "Run, Howie! Run before it gets you!" screamed Ramona. She was mighty Ramona, brave and strong. Howie's sneakers left red footprints, but he did not really run away. He only ran to the next driveway and back. Then the two began the game all over again. Howie's short blond hair turned rusty red. Ramona's brown hair only looked dingy.

Ramona, who was usually impatient with Howie because he always took his time and refused to get excited, found him an excellent Brick Factory player. He was strong, and his pounding was hard and steady. They met each day on the Quimbys' driveway to play their game. Their arms and shoulders ached. They had Band-Aids on their blisters, but they pounded on.

Mrs. Quimby decided that when Ramona was playing Brick Factory she was staying out of trouble. However, she did ask several times why the game could not be played on Howie's driveway once in a while. Howie always explained that his mother had a headache or that his little sister Willa Jean was taking a nap.

"That is the dumbest game in the world," said Beezus, who spent her time playing jacks with Mary Jane when she was not reading. "Why do you call your game Brick Factory? You aren't making bricks. You're wrecking them."

"We just do," said Ramona, who left rusty footprints on the kitchen floor, rusty fingerprints on the doors, and rusty streaks in the bathtub. Picky-picky spent a lot of time washing brick dust off his paws. Mrs. Quimby had to wash separate loads of Ramona's clothes in the washing machine to prevent them from staining the rest of the laundry.

"Let the kids have their fun," said Mr. Quimby, when he came home tired from work. "At least, they're out in the sunshine."

He was not so tired he could not run when Ramona chased him with her rusty hands. "I'm going to get you, Daddy!" she shouted.

"I'm going to get you!" He could run fast for a man who was thirty-three years old, but Ramona always caught him and threw her arms around him. He was not a father to worry about a little brick dust on his clothes. The neighbors all said Ramona was her father's girl. There was no doubt about that.

"Oh, well, school will soon be starting," said Mrs. Quimby with a sigh.

And then one morning, before Ramona and Howie could remove their bricks from the garage, their game was ended by the arrival of two workmen in an old truck. The new room was actually going to be built! Summer was suddenly worthwhile. Brick Factory was forgotten as the two elderly workmen unloaded tools and marked foundation with string. *Chunk! Chunk!* Picks tore into the lawn while Mrs. Quimby rushed out to pick the zinnias before the plants were yanked out of the ground.

"That's where my new room is going to be," Ramona boasted to Howie.

"For six months, don't forget." Beezus still felt they should have drawn straws to see who would get it first.

Howie, who liked tools, spent all his time at the Quimbys' watching. A trench was dug for the foundation, forms were built, concrete mixed and poured. Howie knew the name of every tool and how it was used. Howie was a great one for thinking things over and figuring things out. The workmen even let him try their tools. Ramona was not interested in tools or in thinking things over and figuring things out. She was interested in results. Fast.

When the workmen had gone home for the day and no one was looking, Ramona, who had been told not to touch the wet concrete, marked it with her special initial, a Q with ears and whiskers: She had invented her own Q in kindergarten after Miss Binney, the teacher, had told the class the letter Q had a tail. Why stop there? Ramona had thought. Now her in the concrete would make the room hers, even when Beezus's turn to use it came.

Mrs. Quimby watched advertisements in

the newspaper and found a secondhand dresser and bookcase for Ramona and a desk for Beezus, which she stored in the garage where she worked with sandpaper and paint to make them look like new. Neighbors dropped by to see what was going on. Howie's mother came with his messy little sister Willa Jean, who was the sort of child known as a toddler. Mrs. Kemp and Mrs. Quimby sat in the kitchen drinking coffee and discussing their children while Beezus and Ramona defended their possessions from Willa Jean. This was what grown-ups called playing with Willa Jean.

When the concrete was dry, the workmen returned for the exciting part. They took crowbars from their truck, and with a screeching of nails being pulled from wood, they pried siding off the house and knocked out the lath and plaster at the back of the vacuum-cleaner closet. There it was, a hole in the house! Ramona and Howie ran in through the back door, down the hall, and jumped out the hole, round and round, until the workmen said, "Get lost, kids, before you get hurt."

Ramona felt light with joy. A real hole in the house that was going to lead to her very-own-for-six-months room! She could hardly wait to go to school, because now, for the first time in her life, she had something really important to share with her class for Show and Tell! "My room, *boom*! My room, *boom*!" she sang.

"Be quiet, Ramona," said Beezus. "Can't you see I'm trying to read?"

Before the workmen left for the day, they nailed a sheet of plastic over the hole in the house. That night, after the sisters had gone to bed, Beezus whispered, "It's sort of scary, having a hole in the house." The edges of the plastic rustled and flapped in the night breeze.

"Really scary." Ramona had been thinking the same thing. "Spooky." She planned to tell the first grade that she not only had a hole in her house, she had a spooky hole in her house.

"A ghost could ooze in between the nails," whispered Beezus.

"A cold clammy ghost," agreed Ramona with a delicious shiver.

"A cold clammy ghost that sobbed in the night," elaborated Beezus, "and had icy fingers that—"

Ramona burrowed deeper into her bed and pulled her pillow over her ears. In a moment she emerged. "I know what would be better," she said. "A gorilla. A gorilla without bones that could ooze around the plastic—"

"Girls!" called Mrs. Quimby from the living room. "It's time to go to sleep."

Ramona's whisper could barely be heard.

"—and reached out with his cold, cold hands—"

"And grabbed us!" finished Beezus in her softest whisper. The sisters shivered with pleasure and were silent while Ramona's imagination continued. The boneless gorilla ghost could ooze under the closet door . . . let's see . . . and he could swing on the clothes bar . . . and in the morning when they opened the closet door to get their school clothes he would . . . Ramona fell asleep before she could decide what the ghost would do.

4

The First Day of School

When the first day of school finally arrived, Ramona made her own bed so her mother would be liberated. She hid the lumps under stuffed animals.

"That's cheating," said Beezus, who was pulling up her own blankets smooth and tight.

"Pooh, who cares?" This morning Ramona did not care what her sister said. She was now in the first grade and eager to leave for school all by herself before old slowpoke Howie could catch up with her. She clattered down the hall in her stiff new sandals, grabbed her new blue lunch box from the kitchen counter, kissed her mother good-by, and was on her way before her mother could tell her she must try to be a good girl now that she was in the first grade. She crunched through the fallen leaves on the sidewalk and held her head high. She wanted people to think, How grown up Ramona Quimby is. Last year she was a little kindergartner in the temporary building and look at her now, a big girl on her way to school in the big brick building.

A neighbor who had come out to move her lawn sprinkler actually did say, "Hello, Ramona. My, aren't you a big girl!"

"Yes," said Ramona, but she spoke modestly. She did not want people to think that being in the first grade had gone to her head. She was tempted to try going to school a new way, by another street, but decided she wasn't quite that brave yet.

How little the new members of the morning kindergarten looked! Some of them were clinging to their mother's hands. One was actually crying. Babies! Ramona called out to her old kindergarten teacher crossing the playground, "Miss Binney! Miss Binney! It's me, Ramona!"

Miss Binney waved and smiled. "Ramona Q.! How nice to see you!" Miss Binney understood that Ramona used her last initial because she wanted to be different, and when Miss Binney printed Ramona's name, she always added ears and whiskers to the Q. That was the kind of teacher Miss Binney was.

Ramona saw Beezus and Mary Jane. "Hi, Beatrice," she called, to let her sister know she would remember not to call her Beezus at school. "How are you, Beatrice?"

Little Davy jumped at Ramona. "Ho-*hah*!" he shouted.

Ramona knew first graders could not really use karate. "You mean, 'Hah-*yah*!'" she said. Davy never got anything right.

Ramona felt much smaller and less sure of herself as she made her way up the steps of the big brick building with the older boys and girls. She felt smaller still as they jostled her in the hall on her way to the room she had looked forward to for so long. Room One, at the foot of the stairs that led to the classrooms of the upper grades, was the classroom for Ramona and the other morning kindergartners of last year. Last year's afternoon kindergarten was entering the first grade in Room Two.

Many of Ramona's old kindergarten class, taller now and with more teeth missing, were already in their seats behind desks

neatly labeled with their names. Like place cards at a party, thought Ramona. Eric J. and Eric R., little Davy with the legs of his new jeans turned up farther than the legs of any other boy's jeans, Susan with her fat curls like springs touching her shoulders. *Boing,* thought Ramona as always, at the sight of

those curls. This year she promised herself she would not pull those curls no matter how much they tempted her.

Mrs. Griggs was seated at her desk. "And what is your name?" she asked Ramona. Mrs. Griggs, older than Miss Binney, looked pleasant enough, but of course she was not Miss Binney. Her hair, which was no special color, was parted in the middle and held at the back of her neck with a plastic clasp.

"Ramona. Ramona Q."

"Good morning, Ramona," said Mrs. Griggs. "Take the fourth desk in the second row," she said.

The desk, which had *Ramona* taped to the front where Mrs. Griggs could see it, turned out to be across the aisle from Susan. "Hi, Ramona Kimona," said Susan.

"Hi, Susan Snoozin'," answered Ramona, as she opened her desk and took out a pencil. She untaped her label, printed her special Q, with ears and whiskers on it, and retaped it. Next she explored her reader to see if she could find the grown-up words she knew: *gas, motel, burger*. She could not.

The bell rang and after Mrs. Griggs chose Joey to lead the flag salute, she made a little speech about how grown-up they were now that they were in the first grade and how the first grade was not a place to play like kindergarten. The class was here to work. They had much to learn, and she was here to help them. And now did anyone have anything to share with the class for Show and Tell?

Hands waved. Stevie showed the horse chestnuts he had picked up on the way to school. The class was not impressed. Everyone who passed a horse-chestnut tree on the way to school picked up chestnuts, but no one ever found a use for them. Ramona waved her hand harder.

"Yes, Ramona. What do you have to share with the class?" asked Mrs. Griggs. Then, seeing the initial on the label on Ramona's desk, she smiled and asked, "Or should I call you Ramona Kitty Cat?"

Much to Ramona's annoyance, the class tittered at Mrs. Griggs's joke. They knew she always added ears and whiskers to her Q's. There was no need to laugh at this grown-up question that she was not expected to answer. Mrs. Griggs knew her name was not Ramona Kitty Cat.

"Meow," said one of the boys. Room One giggled. Some meowed, others purred, until the cat noises dwindled under the disapproving look of the teacher.

Ramona faced the class, took a deep breath, and said, "Some men came and chopped a great big hole in the back of our house!" She paused dramatically to give the class time to be surprised, astonished, perhaps a little envious of such excitement. Then she would tell them how spooky the hole was.

Instead, Room One, still in the mood for amusement, laughed. Everyone in the room except Howie laughed. Ramona was startled, then embarrassed. Once more she felt as if she

were standing aside, seeing herself as someone
else, a strange first grader at the front of the
room, laughed at by her class. What was the
matter with them? She could not see anything funny about herself. Her cheeks began
to feel hot. "They did," Ramona insisted.
"They did too chop a hole in our house." She

turned to Mrs. Griggs for help.

The teacher looked puzzled, as if she could not understand a hole chopped in a house. As if, perhaps, she did not believe a hole chopped in a house. Maybe that was why the class laughed. They thought she was making the whole thing up. "Tell us about it, Ramona," said Mrs. Griggs.

"They did," Ramona insisted. "I'm not making it up." At least Howie, sitting there looking so serious, was still her friend. "Howie knows," Ramona said. "Howie came over to my house and jumped through the hole."

The class found this very funny. Howie jumping out a hole in Ramona's house. Ramona's ears began to burn. She turned to her friend for support. "Howie, didn't they chop a hole in my house?"

"No," said Howie.

Ramona was outraged. She could not believe her ears. "They did, too!" she shouted.

"You were there. You saw them. You jumped through the hole like I said."

"Ramona," said Mrs. Griggs, in a quiet voice that was neither cross nor angry, "you may take your seat. We do not shout in the classroom in the first grade."

Ramona obeyed. Tears of humiliation stung her eyes, but she was too proud to let them fall. Mrs. Griggs wasn't even going to give her a chance to explain. And what was the matter with Howie? He knew she was telling the truth. I'll get you for this, Howie Kemp, Ramona thought bitterly, and after they had had such a good time playing Brick Factory, too. Ramona wanted to run home when recess came, but her house was locked, and her mother had gone off to work in that office near all those darling babies.

Ramona was unable to keep her mind on Jack and Becky, their dog Pal, and their cat

Fluff in her stiff new reader. She could only sit and think, *I was telling the truth. I was telling the truth.*

At recess one of the Erics yelled at Ramona, "Liar, liar, pants on fire, sitting on a telephone wire!"

Ramona pointed to Howie. "He's the fibber!" she yelled.

Howie remained calm. "No, I'm not."

As usual, Howie's refusal to get excited infuriated Ramona. She wanted him to get excited. She wanted him to yell back. "You did too see the hole," she shouted. "You did too jump through it!"

"Sure I jumped through it, but nobody chopped a hole in your house," Howie told Ramona.

"But they did!" cried Ramona, burning with fury. "They did, and you know it! You're a fibber, Howie Kemp!"

"You're just making that up," said Howie.

"Two men pried some siding off your house with crowbars. Nobody chopped a hole at all."

Ramona was suddenly subdued. "What's the difference?" she asked, even though she knew in her heart that Howie was right.

"Lots," said Howie. "You chop with an ax, not a crowbar."

"Howie Kemp! You make me so mad!" shouted Ramona. "You knew what I meant!" She wanted to hit. She wanted to kick, but she did not, because now she was in the first grade. Still, she had to punish Howie, so she said, "I am never going to play Brick Factory with you again! So there!"

"Okay," said Howie. "I guess I'll have to come and take back my bricks."

Ramona was sorry she had spoken so hastily. She would miss Howie's bricks. She turned and kicked the side of the school. She had not fibbed. Not really. She had only meant to make the story exciting, and since tools did not interest her, she felt that a hole really had been chopped in her house. That was the trouble with Howie. If she offered him a glass of bug juice, he said, "That's Kool-Aid." If she said, "It's been a million years since I had a Popsicle," he said, "You had a Popsicle last week. I saw you."

Ramona began to feel heavy with guilt. Now the whole class and Mrs. Griggs thought Ramona was a fibber. Here it was, the first half of the first morning of the first day of school, and already the first grade was spoiled for her. When the class returned to Room One, Ramona did not raise her hand the rest of the day, even though she ached to give answers. She wanted to go to Mrs. Griggs and explain the whole thing, but Mrs. Griggs seemed so busy she did not know how to approach her.

The class forgot the incident. By lunchtime

no one called her a liar with pants on fire, but Ramona remembered and, as it turned out, so did Howie.

That afternoon Ramona had to go shopping with her mother. Ramona could see that having to make her own bed and maybe even bake her own cookies were not the only disadvantages of her mother's new job. Ramona was going to be dragged around on boring errands after school, because her mother could no longer do them in the morning. When they returned and Mrs. Quimby was unloading groceries on the driveway, the first thing that Ramona noticed was that Howie had come and taken away all of his bricks. She looked to see if he had left her one little piece of a brick, but he had taken them all, even the smithereens. And just when she most felt like some good hard pounding, too.

5

Owl Trouble

One afternoon late in September, when the air was hazy with smoke from distant forest fires and the sun hung in the sky like an orange volleyball, Ramona was sharpening her pencil as an excuse to look out the window at Miss Binney's afternoon kindergarten class, busy drawing butterflies with colored chalk on the asphalt of the playground. This had been a disappointing day for Ramona, who had come to school eager to tell about her new room, which was almost completed. Mrs. Griggs said they did not have time for Show and Tell that morning. Ramona had sat up as tall as she could, but Mrs. Griggs chose Patty to lead the flag salute.

How happy the kindergartners looked out in the smoky autumn sunshine! Ramona turned the handle of the pencil sharpener more and more slowly while she admired the butterflies with pink wings and yellow spots and butterflies with green wings and orange spots. She longed to be outside drawing with those bright chalks.

At the same time Ramona wondered what Beezus was doing upstairs in Mr. Cardoza's room. Beezus was enjoying school. The boys, as Mrs. Quimby had predicted, had forgotten the Beezus-Jesus episode. Every time Beezus opened her mouth at home it was Mr. Cardoza this or Mr. Cardoza that. Mr. Cardoza let his class push their desks around any way they wanted. Mr. Cardoza—guess what!—drove a red sports car. Mr. Cardoza let his class bring mice to school. Mr. Cardoza said funny things that made his class laugh. When his class grew too noisy, he said, "All right, let's quiet down to a dull roar." Mr. Cardoza expected his class to have good manners. . . .

Mrs. Griggs's calm voice interrupted Ramona's thoughts. "Ramona, remember your seat."

Ramona, who discovered she had ground her pencil in half, remembered her seat. She sat quietly as Mrs. Griggs pushed a lock of hair behind her ear and said, as she had said every day since first grade had started, "We are not in kindergarten any longer. We are in the first grade, and people in the first grade must learn to be good workers."

What Mrs. Griggs did not seem to understand was that Ramona was a good worker. She had learned *bunny* and *apple* and *airplane* and all the other words in her new reader. When Mrs. Griggs read out, "Toys," Ramona could circle *toys* in her workbook. She was not like poor little Davy, who was still stuck on *saw* and *was*. If the book said *saw*, Davy read *was*. If the book said *dog*, Davy read *god*. Ramona felt so sorry for Davy that whenever she could she tried to help him circle the right pictures in his workbook. Mrs. Griggs did not understand that Ramona wanted to help Davy. She always told Ramona to keep her eyes on her own work. "Keep your eyes on your own work," was a favorite saying of Mrs. Griggs. Another was, "Nobody likes a tattletale." If Joey complained that Eric J. hit him, Mrs. Griggs answered, "Joey, nobody likes a tattletale."

Now Mrs. Griggs was saying, "If Susan

and Howie and Davy were eating apples and gave apples to Eric J. and Patty, how many people would have apples?" Ramona sat quietly while half the class waved their hands.

"Ramona," said Mrs. Griggs, in a voice that hinted she had caught Ramona napping.

"Five," answered Ramona. She was bored, not napping. She had learned to think about schoolwork, and at the same time think about other things in a private corner of her mind. "Mrs. Griggs, when do we get to make paper-bag owls?"

Susan spoke without raising her hand. "Yes, Mrs. Griggs. You said we would get to make wise old owls for Parents' Night." Parents' Night was not the same as Open House. On Parents' Night the children stayed home while parents came to school to listen to teachers explain what the children were going to learn during the school year.

"Yes," said Howie. "We remembered to bring our paper bags from home."

Mrs. Griggs looked tired. She glanced at the clock.

"Whoo-whoo!" hooted Davy, which was brave of him and, as Ramona could not help thinking, rather kindergartnish. Others must not have agreed with this thought, for Mrs. Griggs's room was filled with a hubbub of hoots.

Mrs. Griggs tucked the wisp of hair behind her ear and gave up. "All right, class. Since the afternoon is so warm, we will postpone our seat work and work on our owls."

Instantly Room One was wide-awake. Paper bags and crayons came out of desks. The scissors monitor passed out scissors. The paper monitor passed out squares of orange, black, and yellow paper. Mrs. Griggs got out the pastepots and paper bags for those who had forgotten to bring theirs from home. The class would make owls, print their names on them, and set them up on their desks for their parents to admire.

The minutes on the electric clock clicked by with an astonishing speed. Mrs. Griggs showed the class how to make orange triangles for beaks and big yellow circles with smaller black circles on top for eyes. She told Patty not to worry if her bag had *Frosty Ice Cream Bag* printed on one side. Just turn it over and use the other side. Most people tried to make their owls look straight ahead, but Eric R. made his owl cross-eyed. Ramona tried her eyes in several positions and finally decided to have them looking off to the right. Then she noticed Susan's owl was looking off to the right, too.

Ramona frowned and picked up her black crayon. Since the owl was supposed to look wise, she drew spectacles around his eyes, and out of the corner of her eye, she noticed Susan doing the same thing. Susan was copying Ramona's owl! "Copycat!" whispered Ramona, but Susan ignored her by going over her crayon lines to make them blacker.

"Ramona, pay attention to your own work," said Mrs. Griggs. "Howie, it is not necessary to pound your eyes down with your fist. The paste will make them stick."

Ramona pulled her owl closer to her chest and tried to hide it in the circle of her arm, so that old copycat Susan could not see. With her brown crayon she drew wings and began to cover her owl with *V*'s, which represented feathers.

By now Mrs. Griggs was walking up and down between the desks admiring and commenting on the owls. Karen's owl was such a nice, neat owl. My, what big eyes Patty's owl had! George wasted paste. So had several others. "Class, when we waste paste," said Mrs. Griggs, "and then pound our eyes down with our fists, our eyes skid." Ramona congratulated herself on her owl's nonskid eyes.

Mrs. Griggs paused between Ramona's and Susan's desks. Ramona bent over her owl, because she wanted to surprise Mrs. Griggs when it was finished. "What a wise old owl Susan has made!" Mrs. Griggs held up Susan's owl for the class to see while Susan tried to look modest and pleased at the same time. Ramona was furious. Susan's owl had wings and feathers exactly like her owl. Susan had peeked! Susan had copied! She scowled at Susan and thought, Copycat, copycat! She longed to tell Mrs. Griggs that Susan had copied, but she knew what the answer would be. "Ramona, nobody likes a tattletale."

Mrs. Griggs continued to admire Susan's owl. "Susan, your owl is looking at something.

What do you think he's looking at?"

"Um-m." Susan was taken by surprise. "Um-m. Another owl?"

How dumb, thought Ramona. He's looking at a bat, a mouse, a witch riding on a broomstick, Superman, anything but another owl.

Mrs. Griggs suspended Susan's owl with two paper clips to the wire across the top of the blackboard for all to admire. "Class, it is time to clean up our desk. Scissors monitor, collect the scissors," said Mrs. Griggs. "Leave your owls on your desks for me to hang up after the paste dries."

Ramona stuffed her crayons into the box so hard that she broke several, but she did not care. She refused to look at Susan. She looked at her own owl, which no longer seemed like her own. Suddenly she hated it. Now everyone would think Ramona had copied Susan's owl, when it was the other way around. They would call her Ramona Copycat instead of Ramona Kitty Cat. With both hands she crushed her owl, her beautiful wise owl, into a wad and squashed it down as hard as she could. Then, with her head held high, she marched to the front of the room and flung it into the wastebasket. As the bell rang, she marched out of the room without looking back.

All that week Ramona stared at the owls above the blackboard. Cross-eyed owls, paste-waster's owls with eyes that had skidded off in all directions, one-eyed owls made by those so anxious not to waste paste that they had not used enough, and right in the center Susan's wise and handsome owl copied from Ramona's owl.

If Mrs. Griggs noticed that Ramona's owl was missing, she said nothing. The afternoon of Parents' Night she unclipped the owls from the wire and passed them out to their owners along with sheets of old newspaper for wadding up and stuffing inside the owls to make them stand up. Miserable because she had no owl to stand upon her desk, Ramona pretended to be busy making her desk tidy.

"Ramona, what happened to your owl?" asked Susan, who knew very well what had happened to Ramona's owl.

"You shut up," said Ramona.

"Mrs. Griggs, Ramona doesn't have an owl," said Howie, who was the kind of boy who always looked around the classroom to make sure everything was in order.

Ramona scowled.

"Why, Ramona," said Mrs. Griggs. "What happened to your owl?"

Ramona spoke with all the dignity she could muster. "I do not care for owls." She did care. She cared so much it hurt, but Mrs. Griggs was not going to call her a tattletale.

Mrs. Griggs looked at Ramona as if she were trying to understand something. All she said was, "All right, Ramona, if that's the way you feel."

That was not the way Ramona felt, but

she was relieved to have Mrs. Griggs's permission to remain owlless on Parents' Night. She felt unhappy and confused. Which was worse, a copycat or a tattletale? Ramona thought a copycat was worse. She halfheartedly joined the class in cleaning up the room for their parents, and every time she passed Susan's desk, she grew more angry. Susan was a copycat and a cheater. Ramona longed to seize one of those curls, stretch it out as far as she could, and then let it go. *Boing,* she thought, but she kept her hands to herself, which was not easy even though she was in the first grade.

Susan sat her owl up on her desk and gave it a little pat. Fury made Ramona's chest feel tight. Susan was pretending not to notice Ramona.

At last the room was in order for Parents' Night. Twenty-five owls stood up straight looking in all directions. The bell rang. Mrs.

Griggs took her place by the door as the class began to leave the room.

Ramona slid out of her seat. Her chest felt tighter. Her head told her to keep her hands to herself, but her hands did not obey. They seized Susan's owl. They crushed the owl with a sound of crackling paper.

Susan gasped. Ramona twisted the owl as hard as she could until it looked like nothing but an old paper bag scribbled with crayon. Without meaning to, Ramona had done a terrible thing.

"Mrs. Griggs!" cried Susan. "Ramona scrunched my owl!"

"Tattletale." Ramona threw the twisted bag on the floor, and as Mrs. Griggs approached to see what had happened, she dodged past her teacher, out the door and down the hall, running as fast as she could,

even though running in the halls was forbidden. She wove through the upper classes, who had come down the stairs. She plowed through the other first grade coming out of Room Two. She jumped down the steps and was out of the building on her way home, running as hard as she could, her sandals pounding on the sidewalk and crackling through fallen leaves. She ran as if she were pursued by Susan, Mrs. Griggs, the principal, all of Room One, the whole school. She ran from her conscience and from God, who, as they said in Sunday School, was everywhere. She ran as if Something was coming to get her. She ran until her lungs felt as if they were bursting with the smoky air. She ran until her sandals slipped on dry leaves and she fell sprawling on the sidewalk. Ignoring the pain, she scrambled to her feet and fled home with blood trickling from her knees.

Ramona burst through the back door,

safe from Something. "Mama! Mama! I fell down!" she managed between gasps.

"Oh, poor baby!" Mrs. Quimby took one look at Ramona's bloody legs and led her into the bathroom, where she knelt and cleaned the wounds, dabbed them with antiseptic, and covered them with Band-Aids. Her mother's sympathy made Ramona feel very sorry for herself. Poor little misunderstood first grader.

Mrs. Quimby wiped Ramona's sweaty tearstained face with a damp washcloth, kissed Ramona for comfort, and said, "That's my brave girl."

Ramona wanted to say, But I'm not brave, Mama. I'm scared because I did something bad. Yet she could not bring herself to admit the truth. Poor little Ramona with her wounded knees. It was all mean old Susan's fault for being such a copycat.

Mrs. Quimby sat back on her heels.

"Guess what?" she said.

"What?" Ramona hoped for a glorious surprise to make up for her unhappy day. Ramona always longed for glorious surprises. That was the way she was.

"The workmen finished the new room, and before they left they moved your bed and the dresser and bookcase we had stored in the garage, and tonight you are going to sleep in your very own room!"

"Really?" This actually was a glorious surprise. There had been days when the workmen had not come at all, and the whole Quimby family had despaired of the room ever being completed. Ramona's knees hurt, but who cared? She ran down the hall to see the room for herself.

Yes, there was her bed in one corner, the bookcase filled with more toys than books in another, and against the wall, the dresser.

For the first time Ramona looked into

her very own mirror in her very own room. She saw a stranger, a girl with red eyes and a puffy, tearstained face, who did not look at all the way Ramona pictured herself. Ramona thought of herself as the kind of girl everyone should like, but this girl . . .

Ramona scowled, and the girl scowled back. Ramona managed a small smile. So did the girl. Ramona felt better. She wanted the girl in the mirror to like her.

6
Parents' Night

Ramona stood inside her new closet, pretending she was in an elevator. She slid open the door and stepped out into her new room, which she pretended was on the tenth floor. There she drew a deep breath, inhaling the fragrance of new wood and the flat smell of sheetrock, which her father was going to paint when he found time. Her mother had been too busy to find curtains for the windows or to clean the smudges of putty from the glass, but Ramona did not mind. Tonight she was going to sleep for the first time in her very-own-for-six-months room, the only room in the house with a sliding closet door and windows that opened out instead of up and down.

"Ramona, Howie's grandmother is here," called Mrs. Quimby. "We're going now."

Ramona stepped back into her closet, slid the door shut, pressed an imaginary button, and when her imaginary elevator had made its imaginary descent, stepped out onto the real first floor and faced a real problem. Her mother and father were leaving for Parents' Night.

After Ramona said hello to Howie's grandmother ("Say hello to Howie's grandmother, Ramona"), she flopped down in a chair and peeled off one end of a Band-Aid to examine her sore knee. She was disappointed when Howie's grandmother did not notice. "I don't see why you have to go to

Parents' Night," Ramona said to her mother and father. "It's probably boring."

"We want to hear what Mrs. Griggs has to say," said Mrs. Quimby.

This was what worried Ramona.

"And I want to meet the famous Mr. Cardoza," said Mr. Quimby. "We've been hearing so much about him."

"Daddy, you're really going to like him," said Beezus. "Do you know what he said when I got five wrong on my math test? He said, 'Good. Now I can see what it is you don't understand.' And then he said he was there to help me understand, and he did!"

"We're going over to Howie's house after Parents' Night," said Mrs. Quimby, "but we won't be late."

Beezus made a face and said to Ramona, "That means they'll talk about their children. They always do." Ramona knew her sister spoke the truth.

Mr. Quimby smiled as he went out the door. "Don't worry. We won't reveal the family secrets."

Beezus went off to her room, eager to do her homework on the new-to-her desk. Ramona pulled off the other Band-Aid and examined her other knee. She wondered if what Mrs. Griggs was sure to say about Susan's owl would be considered a family secret. She poked her sore knee and said, "Ouch!" so Howie's grandmother could not help hearing. When Mrs. Kemp failed to ask, Why, Ramona, how did you hurt your knee?, Ramona stuck the Band-Aid back in place and studied her sitter.

Mrs. Kemp, who wore glasses with purple frames, was not the sort of sitter who played games with children. When she came to sit, she sat. She was sitting on the couch knitting something out of green wool while she looked at an old movie on television, some

boring thing about grown-ups who talked a lot and didn't do much of anything. Ramona liked good lively comedies with lots of children and animals and grown-ups doing silly things. Next to that she liked cat-food commercials.

Ramona picked up the evening paper from the floor beside her chair. "Well, I guess I'll read the paper," she said, showing off for

Howie's grandmother. She studied the head-lines, making a sort of mental buzz when she came to words she could not read. *Z-z-z-z-z* to run for *z-z-z-z*, she read. *Z-z-z-z* of *z-z-z-z*-ing to go up. She turned a page. *Z-z-z-z* to play *z-z-z-z* at *z-z-z-z*. Play what, she wondered, and with a little feeling of triumph discovered that the *Z-z-z-z*-s were going to play *z-z-z-z*-ball.

"And what is the news tonight?" asked Mrs. Kemp, her eyes on the television set.

Attention at last. "Somebody is going to play some kind of ball," answered Ramona, proud to have actually read something in the newspaper. She hoped Mrs. Kemp would say, Why, Ramona, I had no idea you were such a good reader.

"Oh, I see," said Mrs. Kemp, a remark Ramona knew grown-ups made when they were not interested in conversation with children.

Ramona tried again. "I know how to set the table," she boasted.

Instead of saying, You must be a big help to your mother, Mrs. Kemp only murmured, "Mm-hm" with her eyes on the television set.

Ramona said, "I have a room of my own, and tonight I'm going to sleep in it all my myself."

"That's nice," said Mrs. Kemp absently.

Ramona gave up. Mrs. Kemp did not know the right answers. The clock said seven thirty. Even though Ramona had fought long and hard for the right to stay up until eight fifteen and was now working on eight thirty, she decided that since her parents were not there, she would not lose ground in her battle for a later bedtime by going to bed early to try out her new room. She said good-night and took her bath without using her washcloth, so she would not have to waste time wringing it out and hanging it up. Then she got into bed, turned out her light, said her prayers asking God to bless her family including Picky-picky, and there she lay, a big girl, alone in her bed in a room of her own.

Unfortunately, in spite of pretending bedtime had come, Ramona was wide-awake with nothing to do but think. She lay there wondering what was happening at school. Guilt over Susan's owl grew heavy within her. What would happen when her mother and father heard the whole terrible story? They would be disappointed in Ramona, that's what they'd be, and nothing made Ramona feel worse than knowing that her parents were disappointed in her.

In spite of Howie's grandmother knitting on the couch, the house seemed empty. Ramona thought about how bad she was. She thought about the gorilla in the book in her bookcase and wished she had not. The sound of gunfire and a woman's scream came from the television set. Nothing to be scared about, Ramona told herself, just the TV. She wished her window had curtains.

Although Ramona dreaded knowing what Mrs. Griggs would say, she felt she had to know. As Beezus had predicted, her parents were sure to talk on and on with Howie's parents about their children. Mrs. Kemp would say Howie needed to learn to be creative, and Ramona's mother would say Ramona needed to learn to be responsible like Beezus. There was no telling what the fathers would say, although fathers, Ramona knew, did not spend as much time as mothers thinking up ways to improve their children.

Ramona decided to act. She got out of bed and pattered down the hall in her bare feet.

Howie's grandmother looked up from her

knitting. "It's past your bedtime, Ramona," she said.

So time had passed after all. "I know," said Ramona and could not resist boasting a little. "I have to leave a note for my mother." On the note pad by the telephone she carefully printed:

Come here Mother. Come here to me.

No need to sign the note. Her mother would know who it was from, because Beezus wrote cursive. Ramona left her note on the table beside the front door, where the family always looked for mail and messages. She sidled closer to Howie's grandmother, pretending interest in her knitting, which appeared to be a small sweater of strange shape.

"Is that for a doll?" asked Ramona.

Mrs. Kemp's eyes were on the television screen, where two boring grown-ups were saying good-by forever to one another. "It's a sweater for my little dachshund," she answered. "When I finish I'm going to make a little beret to match. Now run along to bed."

For a moment Ramona had enjoyed relief from her troubles. Reluctantly she returned to bed. She heard Beezus take her bath, get into bed, and turn out her light without being told. That was the kind of girl Beezus was. Beezus would never get herself into the sort of mess Ramona faced. Ramona's conscience hurt, and a hurting conscience was the worst feeling in the world. Ramona thought of the ghost and the boneless gorilla that she and Beezus had scared themselves with the night of the hole in the house, but she quickly squashed the thoughts by thinking how surprised her mother would be when she discovered what a grown-up note Ramona had written. Ramona must have fallen asleep, because the next thing she knew, her mother was whispering, "Ramona?"

"I'm awake, Mama. Did you get my note?"

"Yes, Ramona. I had no idea you were old enough to leave a note." Mrs. Quimby's words gave Ramona a good feeling. Her mother knew the right answers to questions.

Beezus called out from her room. "What did you talk about at the Kemps'?"

"Your mother's new job," answered Mr. Quimby.

"Oh," said Beezus. "What else?"

"The high cost of living. Football. Things like that," said Mr. Quimby. "No family secrets."

Mrs. Quimby bumped against Ramona's bed in the dark.

"Mama?"

"Yes, Ramona."

"What did Mrs. Griggs say about me?"

Mrs. Quimby's answer was honest and direct. "She said you refused to make an owl like the rest of the class and that for no reason you crumpled up the owl Susan worked so hard to make."

Beezus was standing in the hall. "Oh, owls," she said, remembering. "Next you make Thanksgiving things."

Tears filled Ramona's eyes. Mrs. Griggs was so unfair. Turkeys came next, and trouble would start all over again.

"I was sorry to hear it, Ramona," said Mrs. Quimby. "What on earth got into you?"

Ramona's stiff lips quivered. "She's wrong, Mama," she managed to get out. "Mama, she's wrong." Ramona struggled for control. Now Mr. Quimby and Beezus were listening shadows in the doorway. "Mama, I did make an owl. A good owl." Ramona drew a long shuddering breath and described what had happened: how Mrs. Griggs had praised Susan's owl and said she hadn't wasted paste, and how she had thrown away her own owl because she did

not want people to think she had copied from Susan. "And so I scrunched her owl," she concluded, relieved to have told the whole story.

"But what difference did it make?" asked Mrs. Quimby. "The class was making owls for fun. It wasn't the same as copying arithmetic or spelling papers."

"But it does make a difference." Beezus spoke with the wisdom of a higher grade. "It makes a lot of difference."

Ramona was grateful for this support. "I wanted my owl to be my very own."

"Of course, you did," said Mr. Quimby, who had once drawn cartoons for his high-school paper. "Every artist wants his work to be his very own, but that does not excuse you from trying to destroy Susan's owl."

Ramona let out a long shuddering sigh. "I just got mad. Old copycat Susan thought she was so big."

Mrs. Quimby smoothed Ramona's blankets. "Susan is the one I feel sorry for. You are the lucky one. You can think up your own ideas because you have imagination."

Ramona was silent while she thought this over. "But that doesn't help now," she said at last.

"Someday it will." Mrs. Quimby rose from the bed. "And Ramona, Mrs. Griggs expects you to apologize to Susan for destroying her owl."

"Mama!" cried Ramona. "Do I *have* to?"

"Yes, Ramona, you do." Mrs. Quimby leaned over and kissed Ramona good-night.

"But, Mama, it isn't fair! Susan is a copycat and a tattletale."

Mrs. Quimby sighed again. "Maybe so, but that does not give you the right to destroy her property."

Mr. Quimby kissed Ramona good-night. "Chin up, old girl," he said. "It will all come out in the wash."

As her family left her room, Ramona heard Beezus say, "Mrs. Griggs always was big on apologies."

Ramona lay in bed with her thoughts as jumbled as a bag of jacks. Susan's property was just an old paper bag, and who cared about an old paper bag. Susan cared, that's who cared. Ramona could not escape the truth. Why was everything so mixed up? When school had started, Ramona was friends with Susan, and now look at what happened. Ramona had spoiled everything. Ramona always spoiled everything. Ramona, finding gloomy comfort in thinking how bad she was, fell asleep.

The next morning as Ramona left for school, she asked her mother what she could say to Susan.

"Just say 'I'm sorry I spoiled your owl,'" said Mrs. Quimby. "And Ramona—try to stay out of mix-ups after this."

The wind had changed in the night, some rain had fallen, and the air was clean and cool. Ramona's feet felt heavy as she walked through soggy leaves. How could she stay out of mix-ups when she never knew what would suddenly turn into a mix-up? She plodded on, as if she were wading through glue, and when she reached the schoolyard, she stood quietly watching Miss Binney's carefree kindergartners chase one another. How young and lighthearted she had been a year ago! Miss Binney waved, and Ramona waved back without smiling.

When the bell rang, Ramona walked in dread to Room One, where she took her seat without looking at Susan. Perhaps Mrs. Griggs was so busy with her plans for seat work that she would forget about the owl.

Ramona should have known better. Quite unexpectedly, in the midst of Show and Tell,

Mrs. Griggs said, "Ramona has something to say to us."

Ramona was startled. "But I didn't bring anything to show today," she said.

"You have something to say to Susan," Mrs. Griggs reminded her. "Come to the front of the room."

Ramona was horrified. Now? In front of the whole class? Room One turned and looked at Ramona.

"We're waiting," said Mrs. Griggs.

Ramona felt as if she were walking on someone else's feet. They carried her to the front of the room, even though she did not want them to. There she stood thinking, I won't! I won't! while trapped by twenty-five pairs of eyes. Twenty-six, counting Mrs. Griggs. Her cheeks were hot. Her eyes were too dry for tears, and her mouth too dry for words. The silence was terrible. The click of the electric clock finishing off a minute.

Ramona looked desperately at Mrs. Griggs, who smiled an encouraging but unyielding smile. There was no way out.

Ramona looked at the toes of her sandals, noticed that the new had worn off, and after swallowing managed to speak in a small, unhappy voice. "I'm sorry I scrunched Susan's owl."

"Thank you, Ramona," said Mrs. Griggs gently.

Ramona returned to her seat. The look on Susan's face was too much to bear. Old goody-goody Susan. Ramona glared and added to her apology in a furious whisper, "Even if you are a copycat who—*stinks*!"

Mrs. Griggs did not notice because she was saying, "Class, open your arithmetic workbooks to page ten. Who can tell me how many mittens are in the picture at the top of the page?"

The room hummed with whispers as mittens were counted. Susan's cheeks were red beneath her *boing-boing* curls. She was not counting mittens.

Ramona was fiercely glad she had upset Susan so much she was unable to count mittens.

"Seven mittens." Several people spoke at the same time.

"Seven is correct," said Mrs. Griggs. "But let's remember to raise our hands. Now pretend three mittens are lost. How many are left?"

Ramona was not counting mittens either. She looked at Mrs. Griggs, standing there in her pale green sweater with a wisp of hair hanging in front of each ear. She was always so calm. Ramona liked people who got excited. She would rather have a teacher angry with her than one who stood there being calm.

Mrs. Griggs, finished with mittens, had the class counting balloons. Unexcited Mrs. Griggs. Mrs. Griggs who did not understand. Mrs. Griggs who went on and on about counting and adding and taking away, and on and on about Tom and Becky and their dog Pal and their cat Fluff, who could run,

run, run and come, come, come. Mrs. Griggs, always calm, never raising her voice, everything neat, everything orderly with no paste wasted.

Ramona wished she could run, run, run out of that classroom as she had the day before and never come back.

7
ALone in The Dark

Ramona did not run away. Where could she run to? She had no place to go. Each of her days seemed to plod along more slowly than the day before. Every morning Mrs. Quimby looked out the window at the rain dripping from the trees and said, "Rain, rain, go away. Come again some other day." The weather paid no attention. Ramona, who could not wear sandals in such weather, now had to wear oxfords and a pair of Beezus's old boots to school, because she had outgrown her red boots during the summer. Mrs. Griggs wore the same sweater, the color of split-pea soup, day after day. Ramona did not like split-pea soup. Ramona never got to lead the flag salute or be scissors monitor. Number combinations. Reading circles. Bologna sandwiches and chocolate-chip cookies from the store in her lunch three times in one week.

One day the reading workbook showed a picture of a chair with a wrinkled slipcover. Beneath the picture were two sentences. "This is for Pal." "This is not for Pal." Ramona circled "This is for Pal," because she decided Tom and Becky's mother had put a slipcover on the chair so that Pal could lie on it without getting the chair dirty. Mrs. Griggs came along and put a big red check mark over her answer. "Read every word,

Ramona," she said, which Ramona thought was unfair. She *had* read every word.

Ramona dreaded school because she felt Mrs. Griggs did not like her, and she did not enjoy spending the whole day in a room with someone who did not like her, especially when that person was in charge.

Ramona's days were bad, but her nights were worse. At eight o'clock she sat very, very still on a chair in the corner of the living room with an open book, one that Beezus had read, on her lap. If she did not move, if she did not make a sound, her mother might forget to tell her to go to bed, and more than anything in the world Ramona did not want to go to bed. She pretended to read, she even tried to read, but she could not understand the story, because she had to skip some of the most important words. She was bored and uncomfortable from sitting so still, but anything was better than going off alone to her new room. The nights her father went bowling were worst of all, and this was one of those nights.

"Isn't it time for Ramona to go to bed?" asked Beezus.

Ramona would not allow herself to say, Shut up, Beezus, because doing so would call attention to herself. She lifted her eyes to the clock on the mantel. Eight sixteen. Eight seventeen.

Beezus, always her mother's girl, went into the kitchen to help prepare lunches for the next day. Ramona wanted something besides a bologna sandwich in her lunch, but she knew that if she spoke, she risked being sent to bed. Eight eighteen.

"Ramona, it's past your bedtime," Mrs. Quimby called from the kitchen. Ramona did not budge. Eight nineteen. "Ramona!"

"As soon as I finish this chapter."

"Now!"

What worked for Beezus would not work for Ramona. She closed her book and walked down the hall to the bathroom, where she drew her bath, undressed, and climbed into the tub. There she sat until Mrs. Quimby called out, "Ramona! No dawdling!"

Ramona got out, dried herself, and put on her pajamas. She remembered to dip her washcloth in the bathwater and wring it out before she let the water out of the tub. She brushed and brushed her teeth until her mother called through the door, "That's enough, Ramona!"

Ramona ran back to the living room and seized the unsuspecting Picky-picky asleep on Mr. Quimby's chair. "Picky-picky wants to sleep with me," she said, lugging the cat in the direction of her room. Picky-picky did not agree. He struggled out of her arms and ran back to the chair, where he began to

wash away the taint of Ramona's hands. Mean old Picky-picky. Ramona longed for a soft, comfortable, purring cat that would snuggle against her and make her feel safe. She wished Picky-picky would behave more like Fluff in her reader. Fluff was always willing to chase a ball of yarn or ride in a doll carriage.

"What time will Daddy be home?" asked Ramona.

"Around eleven," answered her mother. "Now scoot."

Hours and hours away. Ramona walked slowly down the hall and into her room, which smelled of fresh paint. She closed her new curtains, shutting out the dark eye of the night. She looked inside her closet to make sure Something was not hiding in the shadows before she slid the doors shut tight. She pushed her bed out from the wall so that Something reaching out from under the curtains or slithering around the wall might not find her. She picked up Pandy, her battered old panda bear, and tucked it into bed with its head on her pillow. Then she climbed into bed beside Pandy and pulled the blankets up under her chin.

In a moment Mrs. Quimby came to say

good-night. "Why do you always push your bed out from the wall?" she asked and pushed it back.

"What do we do tomorrow?" asked Ramona, ashamed to admit she was afraid of the dark, ashamed to let her mother know she was no longer her brave girl, ashamed to confess she was afraid to sleep alone in the room she had wanted so much. If she told her mother how she felt, she would probably be given the old room, which would be the same as saying she was failing at the job of growing up.

"We are doing the usual," answered Mrs. Quimby. "School for you and Beezus, work for Daddy and me."

Ramona hoped to hold her mother a little longer. "Mama, why doesn't Picky-picky like me?"

"Because he has grown grouchy in his old age and because you were rough with

him when you were little. Now go to sleep."
Mrs. Quimby kissed Ramona and snapped off the light.

"Mama?"

"Yes, Ramona?"

"I—I forgot what I was going to say."

"Good night, dear."

"Mama, kiss Pandy too."

Mrs. Quimby did as she was told. "Now that's enough stalling."

Ramona was left alone in the dark. She said her prayers and then repeated them in case God was not listening the first time.

I will think good things, Ramona told herself, and in spite of her troubles she had good things to think about. After Ramona had to apologize to Susan, some members of Room One were especially nice to her because they felt Mrs. Griggs should not have made her apologize in front of the class. Howie had brought some of his bricks back, so they could play Brick Factory if it ever stopped raining. Linda, whose mother baked fancier cookies than any other Room One mother, shared butterscotch-fudge-nut cookies with Ramona. Even little Davy, who usually tried to avoid Ramona because she had tried to kiss him in kindergarten, tagged her when the class played games. Best of all, Ramona was actually learning to read. Words leaped out at her from the newspapers, signs, and cartons. *Crash, highway, salt, tires*. The world was suddenly full of words that Ramona could read.

Ramona had run out of good thoughts. She heard Beezus take her bath, get into bed, and turn out her light. She heard her mother set the table for breakfast, shut Picky-picky in the basement, and go to bed. If only her father would come home.

Ramona knew she could get away with going to the bathroom at least once. She stood up on her bed, and even though she knew it was not a safe thing to do, she leaped into the center of her room and ran into the hall before Something hiding under the bed could reach out and grab her ankles. On her way back she reversed her flying leap and landed on her bed, where she quickly pulled her covers up to her chin.

The moment Ramona dreaded had come. There was no one awake to protect her. Ramona tried to lie as flat and as still as a paper doll so that Something slithering under the curtains and slinking around the walls would not know she was there. She kept her eyes wide open. She longed for her father to come home; she was determined to stay awake until morning.

Ramona thought of Beezus safely asleep in the friendly dark of the room they had once shared. She thought of the way they used to whisper and giggle and sometimes scare themselves. Even their quarrels were better than being alone in the dark. She ached to move, to ease her muscles, rigid from lying still so long, but she dared not. She thought of the black gorilla with fierce little eyes in the book in her bookcase and tried to shove the thought out of her mind. She listened for cars on the wet street and strained her ears for the sound of a familiar motor. After what seemed like hours and hours, Ramona caught the sound of the Quimby car turning into the driveway. She went limp with relief. She heard her father unlock the back door and enter. She heard him pause by the thermostat to turn off the furnace. She heard him turn off the living-room light and tiptoe down the hall.

"Daddy!" whispered Ramona.

Her father stopped by her door. "You're supposed to be asleep."

"Come here for just a minute." Mr. Quimby stepped into Ramona's room. "Daddy, turn on the light a minute. Please."

"It's late." Mr. Quimby did as he was told.

The light, which made Ramona squint, was a relief. She held up her hand to shield her eyes. She was so glad to see her father standing there in his bowling clothes. He looked so good and so familiar and made her feel so safe. "Daddy, see that big book in my bookcase?"

"Yes."

"Take it out of my room," said Ramona. To herself, she thought, Please, Daddy, don't ask me why. She added, to protect herself from any questions, "It's a good book. I think you might like it."

Mr. Quimby pulled the book from the bookcase, glanced at it, and then bent over and kissed Ramona on the forehead. "No more stalling, young lady," he said. "You were supposed to be asleep hours ago." He turned out the light and left, taking *Wild Animals of Africa* with him and leaving Ramona alone in the dark to worry about the mysterious noises made by an old house cooling off for the night. She wondered how much of the six months was left before she could return to her old room. She lay as flat and as still as a paper doll while she listened to her father splashing in the shower. Ramona had to think about her eyelids to force them to stay open. Her father got into bed. Her parents were whispering, probably talking about her, saying, What are we going to do about Ramona, always getting into trouble! Even her teacher doesn't like her. Everyone was asleep but Ramona, whose eyelids grew heavier and heavier and heavier. She was afraid of the dark, but she would not give up the new room. Only babies were afraid to sleep alone.

The next morning, as Ramona took her sandwiches out of the refrigerator and put them in her lunch box, Mrs. Quimby asked, "Does your throat feel all right?"

"Yes," answered Ramona crossly.

"Sore throats are going around," said Mrs. Quimby. Since she had gone to work in the pediatrician's office, she looked for symptoms in her daughters. Last week it had been chicken-pox spots, and the week before, swollen glands.

"Mama, I had a bad dream last night."

"What did you dream?"

"Something was chasing me, and I couldn't run." The dream was still vivid in Ramona's mind. She had been standing at the corner of the house where the zinnias used to be. She knew something terrible was about to come around the corner of the house to get her. She stood as if frozen, unable to lift her feet from the grass. She had been terrified in her dream and yet the yard had looked clear and bright. The grass was green, the zinnias blooming in shades of pink and orange and scarlet, so real Ramona felt she could have touched them.

Beezus was rinsing her cereal bowl under the kitchen faucet. "Ugh, that old dream," she remarked. "I've had it several times, and it's awful."

"You did not!" Ramona was indignant. Her dream was her own, not something passed down from Beezus like an old dress or old rain boots. "You're just saying that."

"I did too have it." Beezus shrugged off the dream as of little importance. "Everybody has that dream."

"Ramona, are you sure you feel all right?" asked Mrs. Quimby. "You seem a little cranky this morning."

Ramona scowled. "I am *not* cranky."

"Another dream I don't like," said Beezus, "is the one where I'm standing in my underwear in the hall at school and everybody is staring at me. That is just about the worst dream there is."

This, too, was a familiar dream to Ramona, not that she was going to admit it. Beezus needn't think she dreamed all the dreams first.

Mrs. Quimby looked at Ramona scowling by the refrigerator with her lunch box in her hand. She laid her hand on Ramona's head to see if she was feverish.

Ramona jerked away. "I'm not sick, and I'm not cranky," she told her mother and flounced out the door on her way to another day in Room One.

When Ramona reached Glenwood School, she trudged into the building where she sat huddled at the foot of the staircase that led to the upper grades. She wondered what it would be like to spend her days in one of the upstairs classrooms. Anything would be better than the first grade. What if I don't go into Room One? she thought. What if I hide in the girls' bathroom until school is out? Before she found the answer to her question, Mr. Cardoza came striding down the hall on his way to the stairs. He stopped directly in front of Ramona.

Mr. Cardoza was a tall thin man with dark hair and eyes, and he made Ramona,

sitting there on the bottom steps, feel very small. Mr. Cardoza frowned and pulled down the corners of his mouth in a way that made Ramona understand that he was poking fun at the expression on her face. Suddenly he smiled and pointed at her as if he had made an exciting discovery.

Startled, Ramona drew back.

"I know who you are!" Mr. Cardoza spoke as if identifying Ramona was the most interesting thing that could happen.

"You do?" Ramona forgot to scowl.

"You are Ramona Quimby. Also known as Ramona Q."

Ramona was astonished. She had expected him to tell her, if he knew who she was at all, that she was Beatrice's little sister. "How do you know?" she asked.

"Oh, I get around," he said and, whistling softly through his teeth, started up the stairs.

Ramona watched him take the steps two

at a time with his long legs and suddenly felt more cheerful, cheerful enough to face Room One once more. A teacher from the upper grades knew the name of a little first grader. Maybe someday Mr. Cardoza would be her teacher too.

8

Ramona Says a Bad Word

The more Ramona dreaded school, the more enthusiastic Beezus became, or so it seemed to Ramona. Mr. Cardoza had his class illustrate their spelling papers, and guess what! It was easy. Beezus, who always had trouble drawing because she felt she had no imagination, had no trouble drawing pictures of *ghost* and *laundry*.

One day Beezus came home waving a

paper and looking especially happy. For language arts Mr. Cardoza had asked his class to list five examples of several different words. For *pleasant* Beezus had listed *picnics, our classroom, Mr. Cardoza, reading,* and *school.* When Mr. Cardoza had corrected her paper, he had written "Thanks" beside his name. For a joke she had also included his name as an example under *frightening,* and his red-penciled comment was "Well!" Beezus received an *A* on her paper. Nothing that pleasant ever happened to Ramona, who spent her days circling sentences in workbooks, changing first letters of words to make different words, and trying to help Davy when she could, even though he was in a different reading circle.

Then one afternoon Mrs. Griggs handed each member of Room One a long sealed envelope. "These are your progress reports for you to take home to your parents," she said.

Ramona made up her mind then and there that she was not going to show any progress report to her mother and father if she could get out of it. As soon as she reached home, she hid her envelope at the bottom of a drawer under her summer play-clothes. Then she got out paper and crayons and went to work on the kitchen table. On each sheet of paper she drew in black crayon a careful outline of an animal: a mouse on one sheet, a bear on another, a turtle on a third. Ramona loved to crayon and crayoning made her troubles fade away. When she had filled ten pages with outlines of animals, she found her father's stapler and fastened the paper together to make a book. Ramona could make an amazing number of things with paper, crayons, staples, and Scotch tape. Bee's wings to wear on her wrists, a crown to wear on her head, a paper catcher's mask to cover her face.

"What are you making?" asked her mother.

"A coloring book," said Ramona. "You won't buy me one."

"That's because the art teacher who talked to the P.T.A. said coloring books were not creative. She said children needed to be free and creative and draw their own pictures."

"I am," said Ramona. "I am drawing a coloring book. Howie has a coloring book, and I want one too."

"I guess Howie's mother missed that meeting." Mrs. Quimby picked up Ramona's coloring book and studied it. "Why, Ramona," she said, sounding pleased, "you must take after your father. You draw unusually well for a girl your age."

"I know." Ramona was not bragging. She was being honest. She knew her drawing was better than most of the baby work done in Room One. So was her printing. She went to work coloring her turtle green, her mouse brown. Filling in outlines was not very interesting, but it was soothing. Ramona was so busy that by dinnertime she had forgotten her hidden progress report.

Ramona forgot until Beezus laid her long white envelope on the table after the dessert of canned peaches and store macaroons. "Mr. Cardoza gave us our progress reports," she announced.

Mr. Quimby tore open the envelope and pulled out the yellow sheet of paper. "M-m-m. Very good, Beezus. I'm proud of you."

"What did he say?" Beezus asked. Ramona could tell that Beezus was eager to have the family hear the nice things Mr. Cardoza had to say about her.

"He said, 'Beatrice has shown marked improvement in math. She is willing and a conscientious pupil, who gets along well with her peers. She is a pleasure to have in the classroom.'"

"May I please be excused?" asked Ramona and did not wait for an answer.

"Just a minute, young lady," said Mr. Quimby.

"Yes, what about your progress report?" asked Mrs. Quimby.

"Oh . . . that old thing," said Ramona.

"Yes, that old thing." Mr. Quimby looked

amused, which annoyed Ramona. "Bring it here," he said.

Ramona faced her father. "I don't want to."

Mr. Quimby was silent. The whole family was silent, waiting. Even Picky-picky, who had been washing his face, paused, one paw in the air, and waited. Ramona turned and walked slowly to her room and slowly returned with the envelope. Scowling, she thrust it at her father who tore it open.

"Does Beezus have to hear?" she asked.

"Beezus, you may be excused," said Mrs. Quimby. "Run along and do your home-work."

Ramona knew that Beezus was in no hurry to run along and do her homework. Beezus was going to listen, that's what Beezus was going to do. Ramona scowled more ferociously as her father pulled out the sheet of yellow paper.

"If you don't look out, your face might freeze that way," said Mr. Quimby, which did not help. He studied the yellow paper and frowned. He handed it to Mrs. Quimby, who read it and frowned.

"Well," said Ramona, unable to stand the suspense, "what does it say?" She would have grabbed it and tried to read it herself, but she knew it was written in cursive.

Mrs. Quimby read, "'Ramona's letter formation is excellent, and she is developing good word–attacking skills.'"

Ramona relaxed. This did not sound so bad, even though she had never thought of reading as attacking words. She rather liked the idea.

Mrs. Quimby read on. "'She is learning her numbers readily.'"

That mitten counting, thought Ramona with scorn.

"'However, Ramona sometimes shows

more interest in the seat work of others than in her own. She needs to learn to keep her hands to herself. She also needs to work on self-control in the classroom.'"

"I do not!" Ramona was angry at the unfairness of her teacher's report. What did Mrs. Griggs think she had been working on? She hardly ever raised her hand anymore, and she never spoke out the way she used to. And she wasn't really interested in Davy's seat work. She was trying to help him because he was having such a hard time.

"Now, Ramona." Mrs. Quimby's voice was gentle. "You must try to grow up."

Ramona raised her voice. "What do you think I'm doing?"

"You don't have to be so noisy about it," said Mr. Quimby.

Of course, Beezus had to come butting in to see what all the fuss was about. "What did Mrs. Griggs say?" she wanted to know, and it was easy to see she knew that what Mr. Cardoza had said was better.

"You mind your own business," said Ramona.

"Ramona, don't talk that way." Mr. Quimby's voice was mild.

"I will *too* talk that way," said Ramona. "I'll talk any way I want!"

"Ramona!" Mr. Quimby's voice held a warning.

Ramona was defiant. "Well, I will!" Nothing could possibly get any worse. She might as well say anything she pleased.

"Now see here, young lady—" began Mr. Quimby.

Ramona had had enough. She had been miserable the whole first grade, and she no longer cared what happened. She wanted to do something bad. She wanted to do something terrible that would shock her whole family, something that would make them sit up and take notice. "I'm going to say a bad word!" she shouted with a stamp of her foot.

That silenced her family. Picky-picky stopped washing and left the room. Mr. Quimby looked surprised and—how could

he be so disloyal?—a little amused. This made Ramona even angrier. Beezus looked interested and curious. After a moment Mrs. Quimby said quietly, "Go ahead, Ramona, and say the bad word if it will make you feel any better."

Ramona clenched her fists and took a deep breath. "Guts!" she yelled. *"Guts! Guts! Guts!"* There. That should show them.

Unfortunately, Ramona's family was not shocked and horrified as Ramona had expected. They laughed. All three of them laughed. They tried to hide it, but they laughed.

"It isn't funny!" shouted Ramona. "Don't you dare laugh at me!" Bursting into tears, she threw herself facedown on the couch. She kicked and she pounded the cushions with her fists. Everyone was against her. Nobody liked her. Even the cat did not like her. The room was silent, and Ramona had the satisfaction of knowing she had stopped their laughing. She heard responsible old Beezus go to her room to do her responsible old homework. Her parents continued to sit in silence, but Ramona was past caring what anyone did. She cried harder than she ever had cried in her life. She cried until she was limp and exhausted.

Then Ramona felt her mother's hand on her back. "Ramona," she said gently, "what are we going to do with you?"

With red eyes, a swollen face, and a streaming nose, Ramona sat up and glared at her

mother. "Love me!" Her voice was fierce with hurt. Shocked at her own words, she buried her face in the pillow. She had no tears left.

"Dear heart," said Mrs. Quimby. "We *do* love you."

Ramona sat up and faced her mother, who looked tired, as if she had been through many scenes with Ramona and knew many more lay ahead. "You do not. You love Beezus." There. She had said it right out loud. For years she had wanted to tell her parents how she felt.

Mr. Quimby wiped Ramona's nose on a Kleenex, which he then handed to her. She clenched it in her fist and glowered at her parents.

"Of course we love Beezus," said Mrs. Quimby. "We love you both."

"You love her more," said Ramona. "A whole lot more." She felt better for having said the words, getting them off her chest, as grown-ups would say.

"Love isn't like a cup of sugar that gets used up," said Mrs. Quimby. "There is enough to go around. Loving Beezus doesn't mean we don't have enough love left for you."

"You don't laugh at Beezus all the time," said Ramona.

"They used to," said Beezus, who was unable to stay away from this family discussion. "They always laughed at the funny things I did, and it used to make me mad."

Ramona sniffed and waited for Beezus to continue.

Beezus was serious. "Like the time when I was about your age and thought frankincense and myrrh were something the three Wise Men were bringing to the baby Jesus to put on his rash like that stuff Mom used on you when you were a baby. Mom and Dad laughed, and Mom told all her friends, and they laughed too."

"Oh, dear," said Mrs. Quimby. "I had no idea I upset you that much."

"Well, you did," said Beezus, still grumpy over the memory. "And there was the time I thought toilet water was water out of the toilet. You practically had hysterics."

"Now you're exaggerating," said Mrs. Quimby.

Comforted by this unexpected support from her sister, Ramona scrubbed her face with her soggy Kleenex. "Mama, if you really do love me, why do I have to go to school?" At the same time she wondered how she could find out what frankincense and myrrh were without letting anyone know of her ignorance. She had always thought in a vague sort of way that they were something expensive like perfume and whiskey done up in an extra-fancy Christmas wrapping.

"Ramona, everyone has to go to school," Mrs. Quimby answered. "Loving you has nothing to do with it."

"Then why can't I be in the other first grade, the one in Room Two?" Ramona asked. "Mrs. Griggs doesn't like me."

"Of course she likes you," contradicted Mrs. Quimby.

"No, she doesn't," said Ramona. "If she liked me, she wouldn't make me tell Susan in front of the whole class that I was sorry I scrunched her owl, and she would ask me to lead the Pledge Allegiance. And she wouldn't say bad things about me on my progress report."

"I told you Mrs. Griggs was great on apologies," Beezus reminded her family. "And she will get around to asking Ramona to lead the flag salute. She asks everybody."

"But Beezus, you got along with Mrs. Griggs when you had her," said Mrs. Quimby.

"I guess so," said Beezus. "She wasn't my favorite teacher, though."

"What was wrong with her?" asked Mrs. Quimby.

"There wasn't anything really wrong with her, I guess," answered Beezus. "She just wasn't very exciting is all. She wasn't mean or anything like that. We just seemed to go along doing our work, and that was it."

"Was she unfair?" asked Mrs. Quimby.

Beezus considered the question. "No, but I was the kind of child she liked. You know . . . neat and dependable."

"I bet you never wasted paste," said Ramona, who was not a paste waster herself. Too much paste was likely to spoil a piece of artwork.

"No," admitted Beezus. "I wasn't that type."

Ramona persisted. "*Why* can't I change to Room Two?"

Mr. Quimby took over. "Because Mrs. Griggs is teaching you to read and do arith-metic, and because the things she said about

145

you are fair. You do need to learn self-control and to keep your hands to yourself. There are all kinds of teachers in the world just as there are all kinds of other people, and you must learn to get along with them. Maybe Mrs. Griggs doesn't understand how you feel, but you aren't always easy to understand. Did you ever think of that?"

"Please, Daddy," begged Ramona. "Please don't make me go back to Room One."

"Buck up, Ramona," said Mr. Quimby. "Show us your spunk."

Ramona felt too exhausted to show anyone her spunk, but for some reason her father's order made her feel better. If her mother had said, Poor baby, she would have felt like crying again. Mrs. Quimby led her from the room and, skipping her bath, helped her into bed. Before the light was turned out, Ramona noticed that *Wild Animals of Africa* had been returned to her bookcase.

"Stay with me, Mama," coaxed Ramona, dreading solitude, darkness, and the gorilla in the book. Mrs. Quimby turned off the light and sat down on the bed.

"Mama?"

"Yes, Ramona?"

"Isn't *guts* a bad word?"

Mrs. Quimby thought for a moment. "I wouldn't say it's exactly a bad word. It isn't the nicest word in the world, but there are much worse words. Now go to sleep."

Ramona wondered what could be worse than guts.

Out in the kitchen Mr. Quimby was rattling dishes and singing, "Oh, my gal, she am a spunky gal! Sing polly-wolly doodle all the day!"

Ramona always felt safe while her father was awake. Dread of Something was worse after he had gone to bed and the house was dark. No need to turn herself into a paper doll for a while. Crying had left Ramona tired and limp, but somehow she felt better, more at peace with herself, as if trouble and guilt had been washed away by tears. She knew her father was singing about her, and in spite of her troubles Ramona found comfort in being her father's spunky gal. Somehow Something seemed less frightening.

Worn out as she was by anger and tears, Ramona faced the truth. She could no longer go on being afraid of the dark. She was too weary to remain frightened and sleepless. She could no longer fear shadows and spooks and strange little noises. She stepped bravely out of bed and, in the faint light from the hall, pulled the big flat book from her bookcase. She carried it into the living room and shoved it under a cushion. Her parents, busy with supper dishes in the kitchen, did not know she was out of bed. She walked back to her room, climbed into bed, and pulled up the covers. Nothing had grabbed her by the ankles. Nothing slithered out from under the curtains to harm her. Nothing had chased her. She was safe. Gratefully Ramona said her prayers and, exhausted, fell asleep.

9
Mr. Quimby's Spunky Gal

Filled with spirit and pluck, Ramona started off to school with her lunch box in her hand. She was determined that today would be different. She would make it different. She was her father's spunky gal, wasn't she? She twirled around for the pleasure of making her pleated skirt stand out beneath her car coat.

Ramona was so filled with spunk she

decided to go to school a different way, by the next street over, something she had always wanted to do. The distance to Glenwood School was no greater. There was no reason she should not go to school any way she pleased as long as she looked both ways before she crossed the street and did not talk to strangers.

Slowpoke Howie, half a block behind, called out when he saw her turn the corner, "Ramona, where are you going?"

"I'm going to school a different way," Ramona called back, certain that Howie would not follow to spoil her feeling of adventure. Howie was not a boy to change his ways.

Ramona skipped happily down the street, singing to herself, "Hippity-hop to the barber shop to buy a stick of candy. One for you and one for me and one for sister Mandy." The sky through the bare branches

overhead was clear, the air was crisp, and Ramona's feet in their brown oxfords felt light. Beezus's old boots, which so often weighed her down, were home in the hall closet. Ramona was happy. The day felt different already.

Ramona turned the second corner, and as she hippity-hopped down the unfamiliar street past three white houses and a tan stucco house, she enjoyed a feeling of freedom and adventure. Then as she passed a gray shingle house in the middle of the block, a large German shepherd dog, license tags jingling, darted down the driveway toward her. Terrified, Ramona stood rooted to the sidewalk. She felt as if her bad dream had come true. The grass was green, the sky was blue. She could not move; she could not scream.

The dog, head thrust forward, came close. He sniffed with his black nose. Here was a stranger. He growled. This was his territory, and he did not want a stranger to trespass.

This is not a dream, Ramona told herself. This is real. My feet will move if I make them. "Go 'way!" she ordered, backing away from the dog, which answered with a sharp bark. He had teeth like the wolf in *Little Red Riding Hood*. Oh, Grandmother, what big

teeth you have! The better to eat you with, my dear. Ramona took another step back. Growling, the dog advanced. He was a dog, not a wolf, but that was bad enough.

Ramona used the only weapon she had—her lunch box. She slung her lunch box at the dog and missed. The box crashed to the sidewalk, tumbled, and came to rest. The dog stopped to sniff it. Ramona forced her feet to move, to run. Her oxfords pounded on the sidewalk. One shoelace came untied and slapped against her ankle. She looked desperately at a passing car, but the driver did not notice her peril.

Ramona cast a terrified look over her shoulder. The dog had lost interest in her unopened lunch box and was coming toward her again. She could hear his toenails on the sidewalk and could hear him growling deep in his throat. She had to do something, but what?

Ramona's heart was pounding in her ears as she stopped to reach for the only weapon left—her shoe. She had no choice. She yanked off her brown oxford and hurled it at the dog. Again she missed. The dog stopped, sniffed the shoe, and then to Ramona's horror, picked it up, and trotted off in the direction from which he had come.

Ramona stood aghast with the cold from the concrete sidewalk seeping through her sock. Now what should she do? If she said, You come back here, the dog might obey, and she did not want him any closer. She watched helplessly as he returned to his own lawn, where he settled down with the shoe between his paws like a bone. He began to gnaw.

Her shoe! There was no way Ramona could take her shoe away from the dog by herself.

There was no one she could ask for help on this street of strangers. And her blue lunch box, now dented, lying there on the sidewalk. Did she dare try to get it back while the dog was busy chewing her shoe? She took a cautious step toward her lunch box. The dog went on gnawing. She took another step. I really am brave, she told herself. The dog looked up. Ramona froze. The dog began to gnaw again. She darted forward, grabbed her lunch box, and ran toward school, *slap-pat, slap-pat*, on the cold concrete.

Ramona refused to cry—she was brave, wasn't she?—but she was worried. Mrs. Griggs frowned on tardiness, and Ramona was quite sure she expected everyone in her class to wear two shoes. Ramona would probably catch it from Mrs. Griggs at school and from her mother at home for losing a shoe with a lot of wear left in it. Ramona was always catching it.

When Ramona reached Glenwood School, the bell had rung and the traffic boys were leaving their posts. The children crowding into the building did not notice Ramona's predicament. Ramona *slap-patted* down the hall to Room One, where she quickly left her lunch box and car coat in the cloakroom before she sat down at her desk with one foot folded under her. She spread her pleated skirt to hide her dirty sock.

Susan noticed. "What happened to your other shoe?" she asked.

"I lost it, and don't you tell!" If Susan told, Ramona would have a good excuse to pull Susan's *boing-boing* curls.

"I won't," promised Susan, pleased to share a secret, "but how are you going to keep Mrs. Griggs from finding out?"

Ramona cast a desperate look at Susan. "I don't know," she confessed.

"Class," said Mrs. Griggs in a calm voice. This was her way of saying, All right, everyone quiet down and come to order because we have work to do, and we won't accomplish anything if we waste time talking to one another. Ramona tried to warm her cold foot by rubbing it through her pleated skirt.

Mrs. Griggs looked around her classroom. "Who has not had a turn at leading the flag salute?" she asked.

Ramona stared at her desk while trying to shrink so small Mrs. Griggs could not see her.

"Ramona, you have not had a turn," said Mrs. Griggs with a smile. "You may come to the front of the room."

Ramona and Susan exchanged a look. Ramona's said, Now what am I going to do? Susan's said, I feel sorry for you.

"Ramona, we're waiting," said Mrs. Griggs.

There was no escape. Ramona slid from her seat and walked to the front of the room where she faced the flag and stood on one foot like a stork to hide her shoeless foot behind her pleated skirt. "I pledge allegiance," she began, swaying.

"I pledge allegiance," said the class.

Mrs. Griggs interrupted. "Both feet on the floor, Ramona."

Ramona felt a surge of defiance. Mrs. Griggs wanted two feet on the floor, so she

put two feet on the floor. "—to the flag," she continued with such determination that Mrs. Griggs did not have another chance to interrupt. When Ramona finished, she took her seat. So there, Mrs. Griggs, was her spunky thought. What if I am wearing only one shoe?

"Ramona, what happened to your other shoe?" asked Mrs. Griggs.

"I lost it," answered Ramona.

"Tell me about it," said Mrs. Griggs.

Ramona did not want to tell. "I was chased by a . . ." She wanted to say gorilla, but after a moment's hesitation she said, ". . . dog, and I had to throw my shoe at him, and he ran off with it." She expected the class to laugh, but instead they listened in silent sympathy. They did not understand about a hole in a house, but they understood about big dogs. They too had faced big dogs and been frightened. Ramona felt better.

"Why, that's too bad," said Mrs. Griggs, which surprised Ramona. Somehow she had not expected her teacher to understand. Mrs. Griggs continued. "I'll call the office and ask the secretary to telephone your mother and have her bring you another pair of shoes."

"My mother isn't home," said Ramona. "She's at work."

"Well, don't worry, Ramona," said Mrs. Griggs. "We have some boots without owners in the cloakroom. You may borrow one to wear when we go out for recess."

Ramona was familiar with those boots, none of them related and all of them a dingy brown, because no one would lose a new red boot. If there was one thing Ramona did not like, it was old brown boots. They were really ugly. She could not run and play kickball in one shoe and one boot. Spirit and spunk surged back into Ramona. Mrs. Griggs meant well, but she did not understand about boots. Miss Binney would never have told Ramona to wear one old boot. Ramona did not want to wear an old brown boot, and she made up her mind she was not going to wear an old brown boot!

Once Ramona had made this decision, it

was up to her to decide what to do about it. If only she had some heavy paper and a stapler, she could make a slipper, one that might even be strong enough to last until she reached home. She paid attention to number combinations in one part of her mind, while in that private place in the back of her mind she thought about a paper slipper and how she could make one if she only had a stapler. A stapler, a stapler, where could she find a stapler? Mrs. Griggs would want an explanation if she asked to borrow Room One's stapler. To borrow Miss Binney's stapler, Ramona would have to run across the playground to the temporary building, and Mrs. Griggs was sure to call her back. There had to be another way. And there was, if only she could make it work.

When recess finally came, Ramona was careful to leave the room with several other members of her class and to slip down to the girls' bathroom in the basement before Mrs. Griggs could remind her to put on the boot. She jerked four rough paper towels out of the container by the sinks. She folded three of the paper towels in half, making six layers of rough paper. The fourth towel she folded in thirds, which also made six layers of paper.

Now came the scary part of her plan. Ramona returned to the hall, which was empty because both first grades were out on the playground. The doors of the classrooms were closed. No one would see the brave thing she was about to do. Ramona climbed the stairs to the first landing, where she paused to take a fresh grip on her courage. She had never gone to the upstairs hall alone. First graders rarely ventured there unless accompanied by their parents on Open House night. She felt small and frightened, but she held fast to her courage, as she ran up the second half of the flight of stairs.

Ramona found Mr. Cardoza's room. She quietly opened the door a crack. Mr. Cardoza was telling his class, "Spelling *secretary* is easy. Just remember the first part of the word is *secret* and think of a *secretary* as someone who keeps *secrets*. You will never again spell the word with two *a*'s instead of two *e*'s."

Ramona opened the door a little wider and peeked inside. How big the desks looked compared to her own down in Room One! She heard the whir of a wheel spinning in a mouse's cage.

Mr. Cardoza came to investigate. He opened the door wider and said, "Hello, Ramona Q. What may we do for you?"

There was Ramona standing on one foot, trying to hide her dirty sock behind her shoe while Beezus's whole class, and especially Beezus, stared at her. Beside her classmates Beezus did not look so big as Ramona had always thought her to be. Ramona was secretly pleased to discover her sister was a little less than medium-sized. Ramona wondered how Beezus would report this scene at home. Mother! The door opened, and there was Ramona standing with one shoe on. . . .

Ramona refused to let her courage fail her. She remembered her manners and asked, "May I please borrow your stapler? I can use it right here in the hall, and it will only take a minute."

Once again she had that strange feeling of standing aside to look at herself. Was she a funny little girl whom Mr. Cardoza would find amusing? Apparently not because Mr. Cardoza did not hesitate.

"Certainly," he said and strode to his desk for the stapler, which he handed to her

without question. Mrs. Griggs would have said, Tell me why you want it, Ramona. Miss Binney would have said, Won't you let me help you with it? Mr. Cardoza closed the door, leaving Ramona in the privacy of the hall.

Ramona knelt on the floor and went to work. She stapled the three paper towels together. The towel folded in thirds she placed at one end of the other towels and stapled it on three sides to make the toe of a slipper. She had to push down hard with both hands to force the staples through so much paper. Then she turned her slipper over and sent staples through in the other direction to make it stronger. There. Ramona slid her foot into her slipper. With more time and a pair of scissors, she could have made a better slipper with a rounded toe, but this slipper was better than an old boot, and it should last all day, school paper towels being what they were.

Ramona opened the door again and held out the stapler. Mr. Cardoza looked up from the book in his hand and walked over to take the stapler from her. "Thank you, Mr. Cardoza," she said, because she knew he expected good manners.

"You're welcome, Ramona Q.," said Mr. Cardoza with a smile that was a friendly smile, not an amused-by-a-funny-little-girl smile. "We're always glad to be of help."

Ramona had not felt so happy since she was in Miss Binney's kindergarten. Too bad Beezus had first dibs on Mr. Cardoza. Ramona might have married him herself someday if she ever decided to get married. She reached Room One just as the two first grades were returning from recess. She heard someone from Room Two say, "Ramona must have hurt her foot."

Someone else said, "I bet it hurts."

Ramona began to limp. She was enjoying the attention her slipper attracted.

"Oh, there you are, Ramona," said Mrs. Griggs, who was standing by her door to make sure her class entered the room in an orderly manner. "Where have you been? We missed you on the playground."

"I was making a slipper." Ramona looked up at Mrs. Griggs. "I didn't want to wear a dirty old boot." She had not felt so brave since the day she started off to the first grade.

"After this you should ask permission to stay in during recess." Mrs. Griggs looked down at the slipper and said, "You have made a very good slipper."

Encouraged by this bit of praise, Ramona said, "I could make a better slipper if I had scissors and crayons. I could draw a bunny face on the toe and make ears like a real bunny slipper."

Mrs. Griggs's expression was thoughtful.

She seemed to be studying Ramona, who shrank inside herself, uncertain as to what her teacher might be about to say. Mrs. Griggs looked more tired than cross, so Ramona summoned her spunk and said, "Maybe I could finish my slipper instead of making a Thanksgiving turkey."

"We always—" began Mrs. Griggs and changed her mind. "I don't see why not," she said.

Mrs. Griggs approved of her! Ramona smiled with relief and pretended to limp to her seat as her teacher closed the door. She no longer had to dread turkeys—or her teacher.

The class took out arithmetic workbooks. While Ramona began to count cowboy boots and butterflies and circled the correct number under the pictures, she was busy and happy in the private corner of her mind planning improvements in her slipper.

She would round the heel and toe. She would draw a nose with pink crayon and eyes, too, and cut two ears. . . . Ramona's happy thoughts were interrupted by another less happy thought. Her missing brown oxford. What was her mother going to say when she came home without it? Tell her she was careless? Tell her how much shoes cost these days? Ask her why on earth she didn't go to school the usual way? Because I was feeling full of spunk, Ramona answered in her thoughts. Her father would understand. She hoped her mother would, too.

Workbooks were collected. Reading circles were next. Prepared to attack words, Ramona limped to a little chair in the front of the room with the rest of her reading group. She felt so much better toward Mrs. Griggs that she was first to raise her hand on almost every question, even though she was worried about her missing oxford. The reader was more interesting now that her group was attacking bigger words. *Fire engine.* Ramona read to herself and thought, Pow! I got you, *fire engine. Monkey.* Pow! I got you, *monkey.*

The buzz of the little black telephone beside Mrs. Griggs's desk interrupted work in Room One. Everyone wanted to listen to Mrs. Griggs talk to the principal's office, because they might hear something important.

"Yes," said Mrs. Griggs to the telephone. "Yes, we do." With the receiver pressed to her ear, she turned away from the telephone and looked at Ramona. Everyone else in Room One looked at her, too. Now what? thought Ramona. Now what have I done? "All right," said Mrs. Griggs to the telephone. "I'll send her along." She replaced the receiver. Room One, most of all Ramona, waited.

"Ramona, your shoe is waiting for you in the office," said the teacher. "When the dog's owner found it on the lawn, he brought it to school and the secretary guessed it was a first-grade size. You may be excused to go get it."

Whew! thought Ramona in great relief, as she limped happily off to the office. This day was turning out to be better than she had expected. She accepted her shoe, now interestingly scarred with toothmarks, from Mrs. Miller, the school secretary.

"My goodness," said Mrs. Miller, as Ramona shoved her foot into her shoe and tied the lace, still damp from being chewed, in a tight bow. "It's a good thing your foot came out of your shoe when the dog got hold of it. He must have had pretty big teeth."

"He did," Ramona assured the secretary. "Great big teeth. Like a wolf. He chased me." Now that Ramona was safe in her two shoes, she was eager for an audience. "He chased me, but I took off my shoe and threw it at him, and that stopped him."

"Fancy that!" Mrs. Miller was plainly impressed by Ramona's story. "You took off your shoe and threw it right at him! You must be a very brave girl."

"I guess maybe I am," said Ramona, pleased by the com-  pliment. Of course, she was brave. She had scars on her shoe to prove it. She hoped her mother would not be in too much of a hurry to hide the toothmarks with fresh shoe polish. She hippity-hopped, paper slipper in hand, down the hall to show off her scars to Room One.

Brave Ramona, that's what they would think, just about the bravest girl in the first grade. And they would be right. This time Ramona was sure.

Beverly Cleary is one of America's most popular authors. Born in McMinnville, Oregon, she lived on a farm in Yamhill until she was six and then moved to Portland. After college, as the children's librarian in Yakima, Washington, she was challenged to find stories for non-readers. She wrote her first book, HENRY HUGGINS, in response to a boy's question, "Where are the books about kids like us?"

Mrs. Cleary's books have earned her many prestigious awards, including the American Library Association's Laura Ingalls Wilder Award, presented in recognition of her lasting contribution to children's literature. Her DEAR MR. HENSHAW was awarded the 1984 John Newbery Medal, and both RAMONA QUIMBY, AGE 8 and RAMONA AND HER FATHER have been named Newbery Honor Books. In addition, her books have won more than thirty-five statewide awards based on the votes of her young readers. Her characters, including Henry Huggins, Ellen Tebbits, Otis Spofford, and Beezus and Ramona Quimby, as well as Ribsy, Socks, and Ralph S. Mouse, have delighted children for generations. Mrs. Cleary lives in coastal California.

Visit Beverly Cleary on the World Wide Web at www.beverlycleary.com.